Published by Avalon Books,
an imprint of Thomas Bouregy & Co., Inc.
160 Madison Avenue, New York, NY 10016

Library of Congress Cataloging-in-Publication Data

Benjamin, Zelda.
Chocolate muse / Zelda Benjamin.
p. cm. — (Love by chocolate series ; bk. 3)
ISBN 978-0-8034-7667-7 (acid-free paper) 1. Bakers—
Fiction. 2. Food writers—Fiction. I. Title.
PS3602.E664C46 2011
813.6—dc22
2011005549

PRINTED IN THE UNITED STATES OF AMERICA
ON ACID-FREE PAPER
BY RR DONNELLEY, BLOOMSBURG, PENNSYLVANIA

CHOCOLATE MUSE

A Love by Chocolate Romance

Zelda Benjamin

Pastry chef Maddie Higgins is horrified when her prize-winning torta di chocolate gets a bad review. Choking critics is *never* a good thing, and she loses her job before the scathing article hits the morning paper. Forced to take a job in a friend's bakery and teach a children's evening class to make ends meet, she vows vengeance on the man responsible for her damaged reputation. But when she realizes that the father of two of her students is her nemesis, the charming food writer Brad Angelo, her anger deflates faster than an overcooked soufflé.

Brad, a single father struggling to balance parenting and his syndicated food column, is completely clueless about the trouble he's caused Maddie. He finds her evasive attitude and chocolate talent to be intriguing parts of her allure, but isn't sure he's ready to create a life that might be messier than melted chocolate when their secrets are slowly revealed.

CR...

Zelda Be...

AVALON BOOKS
NEW YORK

Other books by Zelda Benjamin

Brooklyn Ballerina

The Love by Chocolate Romance Series:
Chocolate Secrets
Chocolate Magic

Chapter One

A half-eaten pint of Ben & Jerry's melted on the floor next to Maddie Higgins' sofa. The reality show she had recorded the night before blared on the TV screen. If not for the loud banging on her door, Maddie would still be asleep.

"You in there, Miss Higgins?" Her doorman pounded on the door. "I've got your mail. The mailman said you have to start taking out your mail."

"Leave the mail, Matt!" Maddie sat up, stretched, and shouted at the bolted door. "I won't do it again!"

Before shutting off the TV, she took a moment to commiserate with the contestants. If that one unfortunate turn of events in the script of her life had been part of a TV reality show, Zest's former pastry chef, Maddie Higgins, would surely have been the star.

There were no cameras that night, though, and the unexpected incident had sent her tumbling from stardom. Would the culinary world ever forget her careless oversight? She couldn't. The look on that man's face after taking the first bite of her award-winning torta di chocolate would have made good reality TV. Instead it left her spiraling in self-pity compounded by sleepless nights and an overindulgence in sweets.

If she had only known he had been there to review her most popular dessert, she might have been more diligent. Looking through the little round window, she had watched and waited for the first sign of pleasure on the handsome customer's face.

That's when everything turned ugly. The expected smile of decadent satisfaction had melted into a cough and sputter. No one choked on her delicious desserts. Too late, someone discovered the cause—soap powder mistaken for sugar.

Maddie and the kitchen crew had searched for a hidden camera. They had hoped an inconspicuous TV camera had accompanied the food critic and this was all a setup.

Paul, the executive chef at Zest, had no one else to blame. He dismissed her before the horrific review hit the morning papers. Instead of TV stardom, Maddie found herself an unemployed pastry chef with a runaway culinary muse.

Even though she hadn't actually added the offensive powder, she knew that when the chocolate hit the fan it would be aimed straight at her.

Over six months had passed since the unfortunate incident, but to Maddie her fall from culinary stardom felt like it had happened just yesterday. To help search for her lost muse, Maddie had recently acquired Geraldine, a happiness life coach.

With Geraldine's help Maddie had learned to face her internal demons. However, her desire for revenge against the man responsible for her downward spiral was not so easy to let go.

Geraldine had encouraged her to acknowledge that the time had come to move on. After all, most people forget such events—even the ones that made good headlines.

Trying to put all this behind her had not been easy. Geraldine had suggested some books that might help move Maddie's healing process in the right direction.

Maddie slipped into a pair of jeans, squeezed her unruly curls into a New York Yankees cap, and tucked the suggested book list into her pocket. She retrieved the mail lying outside her apartment door, tossed it inside, and set off for the public library. Maybe she'd find her lost muse on one of the shelves.

When was the last time she had checked books out of a library? She would have preferred purchasing them, but her present state of unemployment left her with little cash for any luxuries.

Inside the library, Maddie found comfort in the musty rows. Holding a stack of self-help books, she proceeded to the checkout desk. Geraldine guaranteed that with her guidance Maddie would achieve results. Maddie's goal was simple: get revenge and make the chocolate nightmares go away. When that happened, maybe she would rediscover her muse and regain her confidence.

"Your card needs to be updated." The girl behind the desk forced a smile.

"Updated?" Maddie glared at her from under the rim of her baseball cap.

The library checkout girl handed Maddie a card explaining revised library rules.

Maddie stared at the list. "When did all the rules change? I don't know if I have two forms of identification."

"Do you want a new card or not?" The girl glanced at the line forming behind Maddie.

Maddie rested the books on the counter and pulled her wallet from her pocketbook. Finding her driver's license was easy, but she wasn't sure she had another ID. "Will this do?" She handed the girl her bakers union photo ID.

While the girl studied the card, Maddie rubbed her forehead. Seeing her bakers union card brought back the reality she was paying Geraldine to help her suppress.

Suddenly, the library didn't appear to be a very good choice. Maddie should have stayed home and finished off another pint of Cherry Garcia ice cream.

This might be a good time to use Geraldine's visualization technique and get back on a positive track. *Think of something that makes you happy,* Geraldine had said at their last meeting.

Maddie had nothing to lose. She closed her eyes and visualized finding one of those rich chunks of chocolate hidden behind a plump cherry covered with ice cream.

That's when the image turned ugly. She was feeding the ice cream to a man.

Not just any man, but the man she had almost killed with her torta di chocolate: Brad Angelo, the syndicated food columnist.

His revenge was just, but did he have to refer to her decadent dessert as the "soap powder torta"? Oh, if she ever met him again, she would find a way to get even.

"Your books are checked out. Here's your new card." The library girl slid the books toward Maddie.

Maddie opened her eyes. She lifted her pocketbook onto her shoulder and balanced the books in the crook of her elbow. Holding her new laminated library card, she felt a slight sense of accomplishment. BROOKLYN PUBLIC LIBRARY—CARROLL GARDENS BRANCH. The card was tangible proof she had ventured out of her safety zone.

One little accomplishment was only a baby step toward getting her life back on track and rebuilding her confidence. Visualization hadn't worked and any positive feelings she felt vanished whenever Brad Angelo's face tumbled into her thoughts. Since starting her therapy, the technique had the same disastrous result. Hard as she tried, she couldn't shake the image. She would have to report all this to Geraldine.

Just before the exit door, Maddie noticed something of interest on the bulletin board. A smiley face chef in a toque caught her attention. The words HELP WANTED sent a mixed message to her confused psyche. Geraldine encouraged her to apply for anything of interest. Any job was better than her current state of unemployment, but Maddie couldn't take another beating. In this city you didn't send a syndicated food columnist to the hospital without retribution.

Glancing at her watch, Maddie realized she had spent more time than expected searching for her books. She tore off the phone number and slipped it into the copy of *Attitude Adjustment.*

Maybe tomorrow she would call. If someone else got the job . . . "Oh well," she said out loud and walked on. That was the way the cookie crumbled for her lately, especially the chocolate kind.

Across the street, a clock in the window of a jewelry shop approached four. She'd have to rush if she wanted to meet Chloe as planned at the chocolate convention at the downtown Marriott. There would be just enough time to bring the books home, fluff out her hair, and change out of her wrinkled T-shirt.

"Okay, Geraldine, here's another step in the right direction," Maddie said out loud.

Chloe Behar with her pink spiked hair wasn't hard to find. She appeared to be involved in a conversation with a local restaurant owner. Maddie decided not to intrude and to brave the crowd on her own. This was her first chocolate show in months. Could she mingle without anyone noticing her?

The flow carried her clockwise around the room. So

far, so good. Familiar sights and smells were tolerable at a distance. A booth to her right seemed to have impressed a group of silver-haired foodies. Nice old ladies interested in a cookbook signing were harmless. Her curiosity edged her closer. No signs or posters displayed any information about the author. The crowd lining up along the wall seemed very excited to meet whoever was at the end. How much trouble could she get into if she investigated?

The line moved slowly, giving Maddie time to soak in her surroundings. She listened to the author, still not visible from her position. He talked to each of his fans as if they were personal friends. "Sally, nice of you to stop by and pick up a copy. Did you try the chocolate meatball recipe?"

Nice voice, seems charming. Did she detect a hint of an Italian accent? Maddie had spent time in Europe after graduating from the École du Chocolat in France. Along with a knack for blending chocolate, Maddie discovered she had the ability to catch an accent after hearing only a few words. The author's accent was not native, but definitely Italian with enough charm and good manners that she felt compelled to move forward and investigate.

The next fan got a similar comment. How nice to hear someone take the time and interest in his reader base. She stretched on her tiptoes for a glimpse, expecting to see a happy, robust Italian chef, but couldn't see over the heads in front of her.

Geraldine would suggest she take the moment and allow herself the luxury of a daydream. The jolly author would find kind words for her too. He had no idea that her muse was gone. They'd discuss his techniques and ingredients. There would be no horrible images clouding this thought. Comfortable that she had picked the right booth to gently ease herself back into the world of chocolate, she held on to the fantasy and moved forward with the line.

Almost there, she reached for a copy of his book.

"Did you find a favorite recipe?" A deep, simmering male voice cut through her thoughts.

Maddie took a second to refocus her attention on the man behind the stack of cookbooks. The unexpected sight of the man behind the desk stunned her. This was no fat chef.

She blinked in an attempt to make the image go away, but the same handsome face was smiling at her. She had no doubt it was the same face she had viewed through the little round window of the kitchen at Zest. Brad Angelo, the food writer responsible for her current situation, stared up at her. She hadn't heard an accent that night at Zest. How could she? The man couldn't speak; he was choking on her dessert.

Run! a little voice inside told her. She couldn't if she tried. Her legs felt like chocolate melting on a hot sidewalk. "No. I haven't read the book," she finally squeaked. This was not how she had expected to act if she ever found herself face-to-face with this man. Over and over she had prepared snippy remarks to make him feel the pain she'd experienced after his horrific review.

The vision of him choking on her torta di chocolate had haunted her day and night since that unfortunate evening. To make matters worse, she had pasted to her refrigerator a copy of his restaurant review. With his headshot in the upper lefthand corner, it was the first thing she had seen every morning. When Geraldine insisted Maddie throw away the review, Maddie made sure she shredded his face horizontally as well as vertically.

How could she have made such a bad choice of booths? Her guardian angel must have run away with her muse.

Brad Angelo's gaze was riveted to her face. She thought he might be trying to place her. Of course he had no idea who she was. He had never laid eyes on her. He probably imagined the creator of the infamous torta di chocolate was some fat pastry chef with a talent for poisoning her customers. Well, almost poisoning.

What was a little soap powder between colleagues? She hadn't even known a critic was in the restaurant that evening. Most chefs preferred not to know. They might try too hard and mess up. As if Maddie could have messed up any worse. What would she have done different?

The memory, even after so many months, was all too clear. EMS had arrived with siren blaring. The handsome man had been wheeled to the waiting ambulance.

Refocus, refocus, Geraldine's voice whispered in her head.

This man with the sexy curve to his mouth was very much alive and well.

"Who should I address it to?" His appreciative eyes traveled from her face to the sagging neckline of her T-shirt. A smile lit up his extremely handsome face.

"Address?" She was fully aware of the message he was sending and regretted not taking the time to change into something more stylish. The undeniable and dreadful truth was that she hadn't felt this way in months. Sitting in front of the television consuming pints of ice cream didn't require the latest fashions.

"Yes. What's your name?" With his pen positioned on the title page he asked, "You want a signed copy?"

"Make it generic. It's a gift for my friend," she replied with contempt he wouldn't understand. She didn't want his book or his smiles. Wandering onto his line had been a mistake. She needed to slip away with as little commotion as possible.

Brad Angelo was not going to let that happen. "Do you work with chocolate?" His polite chatter extended to even those who had not read his book.

"Not anymore." Maddie hadn't baked anything since that horrid evening.

"Why not?"

"Oh, some big mouth had an unfortunate incident after eating one of my special desserts." Maddie answered matter-of-factly.

Brad leaned forward, his piercing dark eyes never

leaving her face. With a playful tilt to the corner of his mouth he asked, "Was it that bad?"

"Not at all. It was actually one of the best desserts I ever made." Should she feel guilt for the way she was baiting him? After all, he had no idea how serious she was.

"That good?" He looked a bit puzzled.

"Award-winning," she retorted.

"What brings you to a chocolate event?"

"I came with a friend." Maddie looked over her shoulder and pointed in the direction of Chloe's pink spikes. Shifting her gaze back to him, she watched him write his number on the back of a business card. He casually slipped the card into the copy of the cookbook she was about to purchase.

"If your friend shares some of the recipes with you, give me a call and we can discuss them."

"Oh, I don't think that will happen."

"She won't share the book with you or you won't call me?"

"I don't read cookbooks." Maddie reached for the book, careful not to let her fingers touch his. She didn't want him to be real. As much as she wanted the horrible choking vision to go away, she couldn't think of Brad Angelo as anything other than the man who had ruined her life.

"That's a shame. Everyone here is interested in some form of chocolate." With an open palm he took in the crowded room. "Everything a chocoholic could wish for: bubble gum, flowers, even underwear."

"Everyone picks their poison." *Oh my god.* Had she really said that? She wanted this conversation to end. Behind Maddie the line had grown longer. What did a group of senior citizens find so compelling about this man? She doubted it was the way his muscles rippled under his white T-shirt with a chocolate bar stretched across his chest.

"Looks like Brad is interested in more than signing this lady's book." A gray-haired gentleman behind her chuckled.

"I think that's a polite way of telling us to move on." Brad flashed a boyish smile and handed her the autographed book. Maddie hesitated, wanting to make some comment before walking away. He had already turned to greet the elderly man. Without a word she walked away. She didn't want to turn around, but just before disappearing into the crowd something compelled her to peer over her shoulder. Brad looked up from the book he was signing and winked. Maddie rushed off.

She had had enough of this. Allowing Chloe to talk her into coming here had been a mistake. She needed more time before she tried to assimilate back into the culinary world. Even Geraldine would agree that coming face-to-face with the man responsible for her current situation had to be bad karma.

Maddie found a quiet corner in the lobby and plopped herself down in an overstuffed chair. Forcing herself even deeper into the seat, she hoped to remain as inconspicuous as possible. She dared to glance at the cover of the book in her lap. A chocolate-covered meatball stared back. She flipped the book over. The back cover photo of the cookbook's author disturbed her even more. She turned the book back to the giant meatball.

Maddie preferred her chocolate pure. What a weird recipe to feature on a cookbook cover. This is a chocolate fair and anything goes—isn't that what Brad Angelo had informed her?

Gently she opened the cover. Her curiosity got the better of her. She began reading the dedication. Who would a cruel man like Brad Angelo find inspiring enough to dedicate an entire book to? Jack the Ripper?

The author would like to thank the chefs and bakers of NY. Without them this book would not have been possible.

"Yeah, right," Maddie mumbled under her breath.

"Talking to yourself again?"

Maddie looked up and smiled at Chloe. "I've been my best company lately."

"What are you doing with that book?" Chloe took the cookbook from Maddie.

"You wouldn't believe the story if I told you."

"Try me," Chloe said, and sat down.

Chloe and Maddie had attended the École du Chocolat in France together what seemed like a lifetime ago. When they'd returned to the States they'd had every intention of being partners in a chocolate specialty shop, until life took them in different directions.

Chloe owned a delightful chocolate shop in Brooklyn, was married to one of the city's most eligible bachelors, and was expecting her first baby. Maddie, still single, had been a renowned pastry chef at Zest, a five-star Manhattan restaurant, until that disastrous day. Chloe had come to the rescue, refusing to allow her friend to wallow in her misery. She convinced Maddie that there was no shame in taking a break from her current position. To keep her in touch with chocolate, Chloe had given her a part-time job at her shop, the Chocolate Boutique. The job helped Maddie maintain whatever was left of her self-esteem but barely covered her bills.

Chloe skimmed through the cookbook while Maddie told her about her encounter with Brad. "Wow, what a coincidence. Talk about having to face your demons. You're going to have to share this with Geraldine." Chloe gave the book back.

"I guess." Maddie shrugged. "Keep the book. I bought it for you."

Chloe flipped to the title page. "You had it signed?"

"Crazy, isn't it?" Maddie sat up straight. Telling the story to Chloe helped her see the irony in her face-to-face encounter with Brad Angelo. "I've got a minimal checkbook balance and I'm spending my money on a book by the man responsible for my current state of unemployment."

"Why didn't you have him write something personal?" Chloe gave her a sly smile.

"Like what?" Maddie gave Chloe a don't-go-there look. "Thanks for the memorable night?"

"That would have been a hoot. Can you imagine the look on his face if he realized who you were?"

"Please, Chloe. He has no idea what I look like." Maddie shook her head to clear the image she had seen through the one-way window of the kitchen at her former place of employment. Surprisingly, the choking image vanished quickly, replaced by a tanned and rugged face with a little dimple at the edge of his mouth. If she allowed the vision to continue it would soon be distressed and ugly.

"He's not so bad to look at, is he?" Chloe said, as if she had read Maddie's thoughts.

"Don't go there," Maddie warned. "I can't handle any more haunting visions of that man's face."

"Well, you're about to get another view. He's coming this way." Chloe stared over Maddie's shoulder.

"I've got to run." Maddie jumped up and absentmindedly tucked the cookbook under her arm. Brad's business card slipped out.

"What's this?" Chloe reached for the card.

"Nothing important." Maddie shifted her weight, ready to make a mad dash for the exit. Why was this man making her feel like this? He had no idea who she was. And even though she had a bad case of hat hair, he had looked at her with those sexy eyes and seemed pleased by what he saw.

He had stirred feelings she usually experienced when she was attracted to a man, or at least a vague memory of those feelings. "He told me to give him a call when I finished the book."

"He did?" Chloe gave her a confused look.

"Something wrong?" Maddie asked.

"It just that he's recently divorced and . . ."

"And what? Did he write a bad review of his wife's cooking?"

"If you met his ex you would doubt she ever got a grease stain on her designer outfits." Chloe seemed to have the scope on this guy. "You realize he doesn't do reviews on a regular basis? The buzz in the industry is that he was filling in for the magazine's food critic."

"Wow. Lucky me. I was a one-night stand," Maddie retorted, then added, "I bet his ex is glad to be rid of him."

"You really dislike him, don't you?"

"Shouldn't I?" Maddie raised a brow. "Why are you so sympathetic toward him?"

"He got dragged through the gossip columns when he was going through his divorce. Some of the photos were pretty invasive."

Maddie understood how Chloe might commiserate with the man. She had met her husband, Ethan, a high-profile real estate developer, shortly after an article about him had appeared in a business magazine. Now, with the baby on the way, they preferred to keep their private life out of the press.

"*He* had a hard time with the press?" Maddie reminded

her friend. "I did too. That doesn't excuse his reference to my best dessert as the 'soap powder torta.'"

Chloe had a knack for changing the subject when she didn't want to answer a question. "Can you work tomorrow at the Chocolate Boutique?"

"Not tomorrow." Maddie hated turning down the opportunity to make a few extra dollars. "I might have a job interview. I'll call you."

Maddie couldn't explain why, but she wanted to know more about Brad Angelo. Today, the first day she had let herself out of the gooey pastry shell she had been wrapped in for weeks, was not the time to press her friend for more information. Her eyes had been bigger than her appetite. She would have to digest all this at her next session with Geraldine before venturing any further.

Brad Angelo was closing the distance between them. Maddie ran for the exit.

Chapter Two

How'd the signing go?" Ed Monte, Brad's book publisher, called bright and early the next morning.

"Not bad. All of my grandmother's friends showed up to buy it."

"If this book does well, would you consider another food-related one?"

"It's a possibility." Brad had been thinking about writing something about kid-friendly eating establishments in the city, but right now he was having a hard enough time balancing this single-father thing.

"What are your plans?" Ed asked.

"To keep my syndicated column alive."

"Anything we might be able to use?"

"Actually I'm working on an idea. It's a series of articles that will revolve around a baking with chocolate class. I enrolled my girls in the class."

"You have no scruples." Ed chuckled. "Using your own kids!"

"Hey, it's not easy being a mom and dad to a pair of precocious seven-year-old girls."

"Does my cousin Dan plan on making this a feature series in his magazine?" Ed asked.

"I haven't run it by him yet." Brad was not concerned about Dan Monte liking his new piece. He gave Brad carte blanche when it came to his column. The Monte family, publishers that provided his bread and butter, liked everything he did.

"I'll put Dan on speaker and you can give us both a hint of what you're up to."

"The class is an interesting concept. It's a generational baking class. The local community center has an innovative director who's trying to keep the place going by appealing to everyone in the neighborhood."

"If you want the girls to learn how to bake, why don't you just send them to Nona's, your grandmother's restaurant?" Dan joined the conversation.

"No way. I was a restaurant kid. I spent my summers traveling through Italy with my parents."

"Tough life." Dan laughed. "But you learned how to make a wicked cannoli?"

He had to agree with Dan; the traveling hadn't been so bad. Brad recalled his favorite memory—a spongy zuccotto filled with almonds, chocolate, and cream. The dessert had been recreated at Nona's and turned out to be a big seller. In spite of the tasteful memories, he had been a serious kid, spending his time at the family restaurant, where he shined silverware and stuffed cannolis every day after school.

"I don't want that for my girls. They should be having fun, not hanging out at Nona's." That had been the one thing Brad and his ex-wife had agreed on—no hanging out at the restaurant for their kids.

Everything else in their ten-year marriage had become major points of contention. The twins had enough on their plates with a mother more interested in her modeling career than her own children.

The Montes, he was sure, had read about his divorce in the local gossip columns. Brad and his runway model ex-wife had started out as nobodies, but as their careers blossomed so did the media's interest in them. When his daughters attracted the paparazzi's attention, his ex took off for fashion shows in Europe, leaving him to protect the girls from nasty photographers.

There had been a photo of his girls and his ex-wife that created some local controversy. The photo had been innocent enough, until it showed up in a gossip magazine paired with an innocent photo of Brad and a carpool mom. Brad was of no interest to the public, but his ex-wife attracted the press. Their divorce had been a mutual agreement, but the photo made it seem like his ex had been the injured party. Even worse, the girls had become the focus of the neighborhood gossips. Brad didn't want to bore Dan and Ed with the details of his custody settlement.

"The headline for the article is *not* going to be 'Kids

Make a Cannoli.' " Brad directed the conversation back to his upcoming series. "I hope to focus on what the generations can teach each other." Brad had built his journalism career by putting a twist on writing about food. New York was a foodie city and his reader base proved it. His article about New York City's top chefs helping to feed the homeless recently won him a prestigious journalism award.

"Have you met the instructor yet?" Ed asked.

"I'm sure she's a sweet old lady from the neighborhood. You know the type. She'll teach them how to make chocolate chip cookies and cupcakes. I can't imagine her not loving the idea of being a weekly feature in my column."

Ed chuckled. "Your self-importance must be what gives you the edge to get the story written."

"As long as we're all making money I don't hear anyone complaining." Brad could hear their soft hums of agreement.

"Want me to send a photographer?" Dan asked.

"No way. I can't chance subjecting my girls to any more sensational photos."

"It was nasty having Sophia's and Emily's pictures show up in the papers when you were going through your divorce. It's unfortunate that had to happen." Dan cleared his throat. "You still blame your old colleague, Simon?"

"His MO was all over it." Brad hated being reminded of how one of his closest friends had not been immune from the monetary reward of such an opportunity.

"Okay, no pictures. If you change your mind, be sure

to let me know. Your public is anxiously awaiting your next column." Dan gave his stamp of approval.

Brad glanced at the clock over his desk. "Gotta go. The first class is tonight and I'm the carpool dad." He hung up the phone. Working from home had proved to be a blessing now that he had sole custody of Emily and Sophia. He would do whatever it took to maintain his literary career and normalcy in the girls' lives.

Maddie sat at the huge round table in the empty classroom. The setup of the all-purpose room worked for her. A small but complete kitchen lined one wall. The other side of the room had a sewing machine, a full-length mirror, and a headless mannequin. The round table filled the center of the room. She liked the idea that she wouldn't have to stand up front and lecture.

All this was new to her, but the director of the community center had convinced Maddie that she was perfect for this position. After all the calls and references she had received from members of the center, Maddie had been her number one choice. Maddie could only guess that after telling Chloe about the job opportunity, her friend had mentioned it to some of the elderly tenants who lived in the apartment building she owned. Many of them enrolled in classes at this center.

The director had been impressed with Maddie's year at the École du Chocolate and was thrilled to have a French-trained chef join her staff. If she was aware of

Maddie's recent job disaster, she had failed to bring it up, and Maddie left it that way.

The cookbook Maddie purchased at the chocolate event would be useful to introduce the concept of baking with chocolate to her class. Although her class would start with simple recipes, Brad Angelo's book proved there was no limit to what could be done with the enticing ingredient.

Geraldine agreed this was a big step for Maddie and she didn't think it strange that Maddie found inspiration for her class in a book written by a man who was responsible for the tumble in her career. The universe helped us heal in strange ways.

But somehow all that metaphysical stuff was not enough for Maddie. She still held a grudge against Brad Angelo and wanted revenge. With her reemerging self-confidence she could stare into those sexy eyes and tell him how he had ruined her life.

That was never going to happen, because she would never see him again. Her little white lie that she didn't work with chocolate was safe. There would be no more careless crossing of paths if she could help it. The satisfaction was hers alone and made her feel better about herself, just like Geraldine had said it would.

While waiting for her students to arrive, Maddie contemplated the weird turn of events. Absentmindedly she stared at the author's photo on the back cover of the cookbook. Brad Angelo's handsome face smiled back. She spotted a marker on the table and thought of the damage she could do to that smug face.

With the marker poised over his photograph, she remembered how much the book had cost her. Maybe twenty-four dollars was not a lot for some people, but for Maddie it had emptied her checking account. Reminding herself of her zero balance renewed her anger.

"Oh, what the heck." She put the marker on his face and started to draw. First, just a simple pair of devil's horns, but the roguish addition just added to his handsome grin. She fixed that with a long, droopy mustache to hide his teasing lips. She was about to complete her artwork with a pair of Spock ears when a male voice startled her.

"Is this where the generational cooking class meets? I'm looking for my daughters." A concerned look knit the man's brow as he scanned the empty room.

"It's you." Maddie looked at the book cover and then the face of the man staring at her as if she were daft. Once again, there was no mistaking the identity of the man standing in front of her. Brad Angelo, minus the devil horns and mustache, appeared out of nowhere. She quickly hid the book behind her back. He had to be in the wrong room. There was an anger management class down the hall. "What are you doing here?"

"Looking for my daughters," he repeated.

"Your daughters are in this class?" she asked, spacing her words evenly.

"Yes. They ran into the building ahead of me." He

looked directly at Maddie. "Hey, you're the woman from the book signing. The one who doesn't bake?"

"That would be me." She hoped he would leave and stop looking at her like they were long-lost friends. "Your daughters may have stopped by the office to sign in. They're probably there."

His glad-to-see-you-again smile threw her off balance. The book slipped from her hand. She bent down to retrieve it, but he reached it first.

Brad glanced at his image covered in doodles and began to laugh.

Not sure if she was more annoyed at seeing him again or that he found her graffiti comical, Maddie grabbed the book.

He toyed with her, refusing to release it. "I like the mustache. What do you think?" He rubbed his forefinger over his top lip. "Should I grow one?"

"It's a personal preference," she said out loud, but silently disagreed. She wouldn't suggest adding anything to his handsome face. "As long as you like the way you look, why would you care what I think?" She tugged extra hard, pulling the book from his grasp.

"It's always nice to get a compliment from an attractive woman." He looked around the room. "I'm glad you changed your mind and decided to read the book. Did it inspire you to enroll in the class?" he asked in his charming light Italian accent.

Maddie could feel the heat rising and coloring her cheeks. She would bet he got plenty of compliments.

Why was he still here? Was he one of her students too? She picked up the sign-in sheet. She hadn't seen his name on the list.

"Are you taking this class with your daughters?" Maddie fumbled with her roster.

"No, no, not me." He looked around the empty room. He glanced back at her, studying her in the most curious way before asking, "Are you *teaching* this class?"

"Guilty again." Caught with her hand in the mixing bowl, she wondered if she had made a mistake taking this job. Geraldine had said if she put herself out there, good things would start to happen. At the moment Maddie didn't find anything that seemed the least bit positive about having another chance encounter with the man she held responsible for her current situation.

"Emily and Sophia Angelo are my daughters." He pointed to the names on her list. A brief touch of their fingertips and she'd had more contact with a man than she'd had in weeks.

She had no one to blame. Being a hermit since the bad review had been her choice. This class had given her a reason to cut her mess of curls, put on makeup, and toss the last pint of Cherry Garcia down the drain.

The man she wanted to hate smiled at her like he might be interested. Was she reading more into it than she probably should? Her fragile psyche felt like shredded coconut.

Maddie pulled the list away and scanned the names. The director had provided a list with the names and birthdays of her students. The class was well balanced with experience and youth. There had been no reason for her to make an association between Brad Angelo and the two seven-year-olds with the same last name.

Quitting before she'd started was not an option. She had signed a contract to teach this eight-week course. She wasn't going to let the presence of this man set her back again.

The library had been her first step toward self-help. The visit there had led to this job. *A point for Geraldine.* Maddie had stepped further out of her secure hideaway and dared go to the chocolate event. Now Brad Angelo was about to become an integral part of her life. If she wanted to move on, she had no choice but to suck up and deal with it.

She extended her hand and cautiously said, "I'm Maddie Higgins."

"Maddie?" He raised a brow.

"Yes, it's short for Madison."

"Nice to meet you, Maddie Higgins." His face showed no sign of name recognition. "If I remember correctly, you said you don't work with chocolate anymore—some incident?" He waited silently for an explanation.

Go away! she wanted to scream at him. "Things change." Forcing a smile, she asked, "What about you? Why does a successful cookbook author enroll his daughters in a baking class?"

"The cookbooks are just a sideline. I write a column for a food magazine. This class concept is a clever idea," he said, then added in a tentative tone, "I'm going to do an article for my column. The director has given her permission but suggested I speak to the teacher before I start."

"To me?" *Oh no, not another article by Brad Angelo.*

"You are the teacher, aren't you?"

"Of course I'm the teacher," she said quickly, to cover an unexplained feeling that her cheeks were becoming cherry cordial red. "We've already established that." Ha, conspiring with the enemy, that's what she'd be doing. He wasn't asking for her permission, just informing her. "What will you write about?"

"I haven't decided yet. That's something I wanted to discuss with you. How do you plan to teach this class?"

By the seat of my pants, Maddie almost said out loud. How long would it take before he realized who she was? Honor and trust were usually big issues for reporters. Would he consider her little white lie a point of contention? That bit of information would give a sharp a twist to his article.

Noisy chatter started to build in the hallway. Students entered and took seats around the table. Maddie welcomed the interruption. How could she tell him she had no lessons planned? He appeared so organized and precise.

"I can see now is not the time to bombard you with questions. Can we meet tomorrow and discuss your background?"

He was so polite she thought he might bow. "I'd rather

you not mention me in your article." She shook her head to emphasize her point.

"We could discuss the award-winning recipe you mentioned the other night."

"Oh, no. I can't." Maddie fidgeted with a random whisk.

"Protecting some secret recipe, Miss Higgins?"

"I've no recipes to protect."

"Something personal you don't want to share with a man you hardly know?" He smiled. "I understand. Maybe when we get to know each other better you'll share your dark secret with me."

She was caught off guard by the sincerity of his comment. He wanted to know her better. She couldn't let that happen. And she definitely had no intention of sharing any secrets with this man, not after what he had done to her.

"Didn't you tell me that someone disliked one of your desserts?" He stepped closer, wedging her between the table and his lean athletic body. "What was it—too much sugar, salt, baking powder?"

"None of the above." She almost choked on her words.

"Perhaps some ingredient to enhance the chocolate?"

"Your persistence is admirable for someone in your profession, but I'm nobody of importance."

"Why don't you let me be the judge of that?" He gave her an irresistible smile. "Everyone has a story to tell. My writer's instinct tells me there's a lot more to you than you're letting on."

"You've never been more wrong." Maddie bit her upper

lip. She hoped he couldn't see how nervous he was making her.

"I'm never wrong."

Giving him a sideways glance, she said, "I'm sure you've made rash judgments in the past."

"Never." His eyes met hers. "So where do you want to meet?"

What was with this guy? Like a stubborn chocolate stain, he wouldn't go away. She lifted her chin and prepared to reiterate what she had just said, but his dark eyes disarmed her composure. Releasing an exasperated sigh, she came up with the safest meeting place she knew. "The Chocolate Boutique on Union Street."

"Great. Mind if I sit in on your first class?"

Her mind told her to deny his request, but something deep inside refused. "You may, but absolutely no questions." She pointed her whisk at him, tapping him gently on the chest.

"Scout's honor." He winked and began to walk toward the back of the room when two identical-looking girls ran through the door. There was no mistaking who they belonged to: From their dark chestnut hair to the mischievous twinkle in their eyes, they were spitting images of Brad Angelo.

Maddie wondered what the mother of these stunning children looked like. Chloe had hinted at a divorce but had not elaborated.

"Emily, Sophia. Where did you go?" A look of relief

crossed Brad's face. "This is Miss Higgins, your teacher." He spoke to the girls but looked directly at Maddie.

"She a friend of yours?" either Emily or Sophia asked, but they were more interested in the goings-on in the room than his actual reply.

"You might say we've recently become acquainted." He took Maddie's hand and removed the whisk.

His touch upset her balance and she grasped the edge of the table. "I've got a class to teach." She directed her remark to Brad and then turned to the students and added, "Everyone please take a seat."

Maddie inched her way to the front of her class. She hesitated a moment, watching him move to the back of the room. His actual presence did not disturb her as much as the force that pulled her attention to the far corner of the room.

Would he still be smiling when he realized Maddie Higgins, renowned chocolate chef, had succumbed to teaching a room full of senior citizens and children? Or would his smile take on new meaning when he realized the impact of his review?

How did the saying go? Those who can't do, teach. Did that apply to baking too?

Chapter Three

Maddie stood behind the counter at the Chocolate Boutique. There were only a few customers so far. The flow would pick up later in the day when Chloe's weekly chocolate cups were placed in the showcase.

To pass the time Maddie unfolded a sketch of the dessert kiosk she had wanted to propose to the owners of her former place of employment. It would have been a small counter in the front of the restaurant, but visible enough that no one could resist buying a treat to take home. She would have changed the contents along with the daily dessert menu. There had been no doubt in her mind that everyone at Zest would have been as excited as she was.

Of course the main item would have been her torta di chocolate. It had become such a hot takeaway item that Zest had created little dessert boxes just for her torta. Every foodie in the city knew what was inside one of those shiny white boxes with the word *dessert* written in six languages.

Maddie released a long sigh. She had no idea what

had possessed her to look at the plans. Maybe it had to do with her new teaching position.

Geraldine constantly reminded her that harping on the past was unhealthy. Maddie was trying hard to live in the present and plan for her future. Teaching at the local community center was not why she had attended the École du Chocolate.

She folded the plans neatly and placed them back in her pocketbook before turning her attention to the display case in front of her. Chloe would be here soon and would need room for her chocolate cups.

Maddie was rearranging the chocolates in the case when Brad came in. He walked toward her.

She looked up for a moment. He smiled and she felt a strange flutter in the pit of her stomach. "Hi. I'll be with you in a minute." She breathed deep, expecting the mixed aroma of the spicy chocolate she had just rearranged to help her refocus.

Instead she picked up a strong, masculine scent with a base note of patchouli. She thought hard for a moment, concentrating on Brad's spicy scent, and tried to place the brand. It was nothing she recognized. He smelled like a walk in the forest after a rainstorm.

"Your aftershave . . . I can't identify it." A warning voice whispered in her head, *Don't get so personal.* But his scent intrigued her.

"It's a soap. I have a great-aunt in Tuscany who has been making it for years. She sends me a case every year for my birthday."

Who was this man who washed with a soap sent to him by his Italian aunt? The same man who was about to try and uncover her chocolate-covered secret.

"Do you like the scent?"

"It's clean and fresh." She thought for a moment. "I can smell the patchouli and a hint of sandalwood."

"You have a remarkable talent." A sincere smile lit his face.

Some talent. If she had only taken a final sniff of her torta the night he had been at Zest, she would have detected something was wrong. "I found it useful when I worked with chocolate," she confessed. What was with this man and soap? Now she had another soap moment to associate with him, definitely more pleasant than the image of him choking on her torta.

"The secret recipe?" His accent, velvet edged and enticing, made her tingle.

"I told you there is no secret recipe." She had already told him more than he needed to know. Her concentration was gone. She pushed aside the jellies she had been working on and rearranged another tray of chocolates.

"Sorry. I didn't mean to distract you." He flashed an apologetic smile. "Nice-looking candies." He watched her nervous fingers rearrange the rows of chocolate.

Why did he have to be so attentive and kind? Where was the monster who had destroyed her career? She forced a smile. Not a special smile, just a smile that she would give any other customer. "Want to try one?"

"What's in that one?" He pointed to a triangular-shaped dark chocolate.

She wrinkled her nose and said, "I don't think that's your best choice." She considered asking some questions, but decided instead to use her own judgment. She would select a candy based on what she already knew about him.

Triangular chocolate lovers seldom worried about other people's feelings. After observing the way he treated the senior citizens at the book signing, she felt correct in assuming he had a compassionate side. He might not be tolerant of tortas covered in soap powder, but he definitely was more than considerate to his fans and daughters.

"Try this. You'll like it better." She handed him an oval-shaped candy. This shape suited him better. Oval lovers knew the right words for the right occasion.

"How do you know so much about scents, candy shapes, and matching people to chocolate?" he asked. "Just a few evenings ago you told me you had no interest in chocolate." He took the chocolate she offered. "Then I find you teaching a chocolate baking class and working at this wonderful shop."

"Maybe I overreacted a little. I've worked with chocolate in the past," she answered cautiously, not sure if he was prying for information. All reporters had different techniques for getting the scoop. Okay, so he wasn't working on a high-profile story, but he did have a large following. Anything he wrote could be and had been held against her.

"Want to try another?" she offered, hoping to divert his attention to the chocolate. "What's your favorite filling?"

"Raspberry?" he said, making it sound more like a question than a definite choice.

"Yes. You could be a raspberry."

"And what would make me a raspberry?"

"You seem committed. I saw your concern for your daughters." Maddie didn't want to get too personal. "Raspberry lovers are family-oriented people." Silently she celebrated her triumph for matching the right chocolate in spite of the little knowledge she had.

Brad wanted to know more. "Anything else?" he asked.

"Well, raspberries don't like complications in their relationships." She gave him a quizzical look and waited for his answer.

"Who does?" He joined her behind the counter and turned his attention away from the candy. "Very interesting collection." He reached up to touch a Mayan bowl hanging on the wall.

"Don't touch." Maddie placed a tray of raspberry candies on the counter. She was not about to find out if there was any truth in what Chloe had told her about the mystical power in the artifacts. Sharing such an experience would be reserved for someone she liked a little more than the man standing in front of her.

Brad turned to face her. "Where does this display come from?" He looked at her with more than just a reporter's interest.

"The artifacts belong to Chloe Behar, the shop owner.

Her parents are archaeologists. They send her relics related to chocolate and she puts them on display." Maddie took note of his restless energy and his interest in whatever she seemed to say.

"What else do you know about these bowls?" He moved along the wall standing much too close to her.

Trying to ignore the odd sensation simmering through her, Maddie reached for another tray of raspberry-filled candies. "I'm sure Chloe would be happy to tell you about the bowls. She'll be here soon."

"Mayan chocolate bowls in a modern chocolate shop could make for an interesting topic." Brad reached over her shoulder, brushing the back of his hand across her bare arm. He jotted some notes on a paper napkin he lifted off the counter. "Have you used any of the apparatuses?"

"I have a *molinillo* at home." His innocent gesture had left her skin warm. She shouldn't be reacting like this. Aside from everything else, he was the father of two of her students.

"A *what?*" Most people reacted just like Brad when they first heard the word.

"A *molinillo*." Being informative and friendly couldn't hurt. "It's a twisted wooden stick. We use it to froth hot chocolate."

"Maybe you could bring it to your class. I'm curious to see how it works." His eyebrows arched mischievously. "And I love hot chocolate."

"What a great idea." Had she given Brad Angelo an

indirect compliment? She had her next lesson planned thanks to him. The man was good for something.

"Is it safe to assume that you're a seat-of-the-pants kind of teacher?" He raised a quizzical brow. "No lesson plans?"

"This is not an Ivy League class in chocolate making." He had to be kidding. Or was this his way of digging for information? "Are you planning on enrolling?"

"I don't have time for many extra activities. I'm a single parent. My writing schedule and my girls keep me busy."

In reality, he appeared open and honest. She wanted to believe him, but experience warned her to be wary. One slip and she'd find herself at the mercy of his pen. She'd kill him with kindness. Well, not really kill him. After all, she had already come close to doing that.

"You deserve a treat for helping the teacher. Why don't you try a different twist on the raspberry filling?" She pointed out several chocolates filled with chunky nuts as well as raspberry.

"I'm always open to new things." He grabbed the closest candy. "What's your favorite?"

Maddie hesitated, not ready to mix so intimately with Brad Angelo. She pointed to a raspberry-pecan candy. "Try it."

"Do raspberries and pecans complement each other?" His question laced with his charm tantalized more than her palate.

"The combination will mesmerize you." She wanted

him to like it, to be impressed with her ability to match the candy to his personality. After all, there was much more to her than her soap powder torta. She just wasn't ready to let him in on it. "Tell me what you think."

"I think you and this wonderful shop have sidetracked me from my reason for being here." He picked up the chocolate and walked over to an empty table. "Let's talk about you."

"Not me. My class," she adamantly reminded him. "If you want to ask me about the class, you must promise to never mention me in your article."

"Okay, I promise to never use the name Maddie Higgins."

"And no photos."

"I don't do photos when my girls are involved. So don't worry about your picture showing up in the post office." Brad laughed. "Are you in some kind of secret chocolate protection program?"

"Yes, that's it." She couldn't help but laugh. She sat down across from him and watched him unwrap the candy. What would he do with the wrapper? Some people were folders, in no rush to be anywhere. Others were twisters who were jumpy, but Brad was a smoother, a massager.

"Have you read my column?" he asked.

"Your column?" She watched his fingertips smooth the foil until it was perfectly flat. The gesture sent shivers down her back. "I've read it occasionally."

"You're not a fan?" He gave her a mock frown,

producing an upside-down dimple at the corner of his mouth.

She left out the fact that she had started reading his column shortly after her bad review. Misery loved company and she had wanted to know she wasn't alone.

"What did you think?"

"Not bad." Surprisingly, she liked his writing. There were times she felt he had his finger on the pulse of the New York culinary scene. Another surprise was the non-existence of another restaurant review, either good or bad. It had been her luck that he was at Zest on that unfortu-nate night.

"Which article did you read."

"I liked the one about the top chefs and the home-less." She wanted to add she would have been glad to be part of their project if she had been employed.

"It was a pretty popular piece," he stated matter-of-factly.

"Do you ever write articles that are not so popular?"

"Sometimes." He shrugged. "A piece might upset some people, but that kind of story makes for good reading." He gave her a curious glance. "Did you find something I wrote offensive?"

Oh my god. He had put her on the spot, and she de-served it. She was always probing, looking for the man she wanted to hate, the man who had ordered the wrong dessert on the wrong night. Searching for words that wouldn't force her to admit she had any reason to find his writing hurtful, she once again changed the subject.

"Don't you want to taste your chocolate?"

"We're never going to get this interview started if you keep distracting me with such offers." He looked at her while he bit into the candy.

She waited for that smile of satisfaction and a glimpse of his dimple.

There was no smile, no dimple. His olive skin turned pale. He didn't take another bite. Instead he cleared his throat.

"Are you okay?" Maddie jumped up, about to panic. She forced herself to remain calm. It couldn't be happening again, not right in front of her. "Do you need a drink?"

"Water would be fine." His palm moved along his throat.

The nightmare images of that night at Zest surfaced. "Not again," she said without thinking.

"This has happened before?" He managed a hoarse whisper.

"No, never here." Was it too late? Could the idea already be planted in his reporter's mind? "Chloe's chocolates don't stick in anyone's throat. They melt on the back of your tongue and slide down like a decadent treat." There was no way Brad Angelo had chocolate stuck in his throat. "What did you do?" she asked, accusing him of sabotaging the experience.

"I took a bite of this chocolate." He pointed to the half-eaten candy. This time he was the accuser. "What was in it?"

"You must be allergic to chocolate." She watched him swallow the water with no relief.

"Never." He shook his head.

"Raspberries?" She felt her composure melting.

He didn't speak, just continued to clear his throat.

"Pecans?" she asked, desperate to find a reason for his present state.

Maddie glanced at the chocolate Hershey's Kiss clock on the wall. Vital minutes were ticking away. Chloe would be here soon, but Maddie had to do something—fast.

Brad's face became redder and redder. Oh no, were his lips beginning to swell?

"Give me the keys to your car. I'm taking you to the emergency room. You're having an allergic reaction to one of the ingredients in the candy." She kept chattering as she led him to the door. "It has nothing to do with the who's or what's or how the candy was made."

He reached in his pocket, took out his keys, and tossed them to Maddie.

She caught the key ring in midair. *"Daisy Duck?"* She glanced at the key chain and then toward Brad.

"A gift from my girls," Brad managed to answer before making repeated sounds that signaled he was having difficulty swallowing.

Chloe walked through the front door just as they were walking out. A quick glance from Brad to Maddie left her speechless.

"I'll explain later." Maddie followed Brad out the door.

Chloe nodded and let them pass.

"Stay calm," Maddie said, more for her own benefit. Information she had read in health magazines flooded through her mind. "A family history of allergies or repeated exposure can trigger a reaction." She said anything she could think of so she wouldn't have to remember the last time she had seen that look on his face.

Chapter Four

It had to be the raspberries or the nuts, anything but the chocolate. The truth was, they might never find out.

Ugly red blotches completely covered Brad's neck by the time they arrived at County Hospital. Scenes like this were always so funny in the movies, but Maddie wasn't laughing.

When Brad recovered, and now that they were at the hospital Maddie was sure he would, would he write a bad review on the Chocolate Boutique? Even if he attributed the incident to an allergy, any mention of the shop in such an article would leave his readers with a negative image. Maddie knew all about such images; she still couldn't get them to go away.

With the flick of his pen he could destroy a neighborhood institution that had been in business for decades. It would be her fault. People in this close-knit neighborhood would talk about her for years. Maddie Higgins poisoned the food writer. The Chocolate Boutique would

Maddie couldn't risk having Alex slip. for her arm, stopping her before she entered. "He has no clue who I am or that it was sent him to the hospital last time."

have to close its doors. She would lose her friends and have to move away. Where would she go?

Why had she wanted to impress him? He was the man she wanted to get back at, but not like this. Why did she insist he try a raspberry nut blend when he had said he preferred a plain raspberry-filled chocolate?

The triage nurse, Alex Simone, was a friend of Maddie's. However, Maddie wasn't sure if she was glad to see Alex under these circumstances. Alex's grandfather, Max, had been the original owner of the Chocolate Boutique. His chocolate secrets had been passed down to his granddaughter, Alex, and his assistant, Chloe. For years the store thrived on the recipes made with those closely guarded secrets. Maddie was sure she had just destroyed a decades-old reputation for selling fine chocolate.

Alex knew all the details of Maddie's horrid review and did a double take when she read Brad's name. She gave Maddie a what's-going-on look. Maddie put a finger to her lips and Alex took the hint. Turning her attention back to the rash erupting on Brad's neck, Alex started asking the necessary questions.

"Any allergies?"

"None that I'm aware of," Brad replied in a hoarse voice.

Maddie felt compelled to explain. "I think it might have been the raspberry filling or maybe it was the chocolate." She released an exasperated sigh. "Or maybe it was the nuts."

"Hey, let the nurse do her job," Brad whispered.

"Any problems in the past?" Alex asked.

Maddie pressed her eyes closed and waited for Brad to tell his nurse how he had almost choked to death on a torta di chocolate made by some careless chef.

"I've eaten raspberries and chocolate my entire life and never had a problem."

He was right. The chocolate had nothing to do with his reaction last time; it was the soap powder.

"Could be anything. Lots of people have nut allergies." Alex picked up the chart and signaled for Maddie to follow. She wheeled Brad to the back, where a paramedic helped him onto a stretcher.

Alex disappeared with the wheelchair, and Maddie waited outside the curtain while the doctor examined Brad. Unsure if she should leave or stick around, she paced back and forth outside the room.

"Mrs. Angelo," the doctor said.

"Oh, no, she's not Mrs. Angelo." Alex approached with medications in her hand.

"I'm . . ." She hesitated, unsure of how to explain her connection to Brad.

"Whatever your association with Mr. Angelo, he has you to thank for seeking such prompt treatment." The doctor scribbled orders on a chart and handed it to Alex.

Maddie couldn't risk having Alex slip. She reached for her arm, stopping her before she entered the room. "He has no clue who I am or that it was my torta that sent him to the hospital last time."

"Okay, but you're going to have to tell me later what you're doing with Brad Angelo. Isn't he the critic who wrote your bad review?"

"He's not really a food critic." Maddie realized she was beginning to see him less and less like the monster she had imagined him to be.

"Your secret is safe with me." Alex gave her a conspiratorial wink.

"Call Chloe. Tell her not to worry. She kinda walked in at the end of this mess."

"I'll call her on my lunch break." Alex walked into the room to give Brad a shot.

Maddie got the feeling Alex was not bothered by Brad's reaction to one of Chloe's chocolates or the implications this event could have on the future of the Chocolate Boutique. Maddie would make it her mission to see that Brad did not write anything damaging about the shop.

Maddie peeked behind the curtain. After a couple of oral doses of medications and an injection Brad looked much better. His eyes were closed and he looked a little tired and flushed. She decided it was safe to enter. She rested her sweaty hand on the cool metal rail of the stretcher. Unsure if she should disturb him, she searched his face for any remaining signs of the adverse reaction.

Brad opened his eyes and smiled. "Hi. Thanks." The look on his face mingled with gratitude and the effects of his medication.

He glanced at the clock on the wall and placed his hand over Maddie's.

Strangely, she liked the feel of his hand on hers and didn't pull away.

"I hate to ask you this. I have to pick the girls up from school in an hour. The doctor says I can't drive." He lifted himself up on his elbows.

The wide armholes of the hideous hospital gown offered Maddie a view of a nice athletic physique. The despised Brad Angelo was becoming more and more suspiciously fascinating.

"It's a big imposition, but if you could stick around a little longer and drive me to their school, I'd be forever grateful."

Sticking close to Brad the rest of the day might be a good idea, especially if she wanted to prevent him from sharing his near-death experience with his readers.

"You could drop us off at my grandmother's restaurant, Nona's on Atlantic Avenue. Someone will drive us home from there. You've heard of the place?"

Maddie nodded. Who hadn't heard of Nona's? However, she wasn't thinking of the wonderful cannolis the restaurant was famous for. Imagine, Brad Angelo eternally grateful to Maddie Higgins. She almost laughed at the absurdity. How could she refuse?

Chapter Five

A couple of late lunch diners lingered over coffee when Maddie, Brad, and the girls arrived at Nona's. An uneasy feeling swept over Maddie. It had been a while since she had stepped into a restaurant, as a diner or an employee. Aside from not being in the financial position to eat out, she had been wary of running into anyone who might recognize her. Any comment on her mishap would have easily sent her over the edge. Chinese takeout and salad bars had become her dining favorites. How sad for a talented pastry chef to fear restaurants.

Emily and Sophia, however, had no reservations whatsoever. They ran through the restaurant announcing their arrival in loud voices.

A lady with whipped cream puffs of white hair sticking out of a hairnet came to greet them. Encompassing the girls in a big affectionate hug, she glanced toward the door and asked, "How did you get here?"

"Daddy and his new friend, Miss Maddie, picked us

up from school," the girls responded in unison, as if Maddie picking them up was an everyday happening.

Brad *was* divorced and might just have a slew of girlfriends who ran errands for him and his daughters. Of course, Maddie didn't know for sure if that was the case. Finding fault with him was easier than admitting his intentions were noble.

"New friend?" The lady in the hairnet glanced in Maddie's direction.

This had to be Nona. Maddie managed a small wave and cautiously walked further into the restaurant behind Brad. Forcing her features into a more relaxed expression, she offered a brief explanation of what had happened.

Nona listened as Maddie explained the events of the morning. Her concern for her grandson was evident, but her joy in seeing the girls seemed to push aside her worry. "You're just in time to help stuff some cannolis. Come, everyone into the kitchen."

The twins rushed off with Brad behind them.

Maddie did not follow. She couldn't get herself to walk into the restaurant kitchen. How many weeks had it been—four, five? No, six months had passed since she had been expelled from the kitchen at Zest.

Brad held the door open. "C'mon. We don't bite." Releasing his hold on it, he reached for her hand and pulled her in.

The swinging door came back at them. Maddie stumbled and awkwardly leaned against Brad's chest. The scent of his Italian aunt's homemade soap filled her senses while his closeness surprised her with an unexpected delicious shudder.

Behind them, strategically positioned staff chopped and ground ingredients and prepared for the dinner rush. The disturbance at the door broke their rhythm. All activity halted. She and Brad became the focus of their attention.

Unaware of the commotion they were causing, Brad put his hands on her shoulders to steady her. Frantic that the staff would get the wrong idea about their relationship, Maddie attempted to pull away. Brad appeared reluctant to release her and ran his hand along her upper arms. The simple gesture sent her heart racing.

Maddie had to get away. She was about to make up some reasonable excuse when a man in a tall chef hat appeared. He would be the executive chef. This was his kitchen and any intruders would have to be welcomed by him.

"Hi, I'm Tony, Brad's uncle and the guy in charge around here." Behind him, Nona grunted. "That is, when Nona's not around."

Maddie wanted to compliment him on his clean, well-organized kitchen, but couldn't risk being found out. Only someone who had worked in a hectic kitchen would know the executive chef called all the shots and scrutinized every movement.

A young woman with spiked hair looked up from the pastry table. She smiled at Brad and the girls. She did a double take when she noticed Maddie.

"Hi, I'm Lily, the pastry chef." She greeted Maddie with a look of recognition. "I know you, don't I?"

Maddie swallowed hard trying to keep the quiver from her voice. "Oh, I doubt it." She wasn't sure of much lately, but the pastry chef with hair like spiky frosting would be someone she would remember meeting. On the other hand, it was quite possible Lily had been familiar with Maddie's work. The heat from the kitchen was starting to affect her. She felt her cheeks flushing. She couldn't be found out, especially now.

"Are you okay?" Lily, completely unsuspecting of the effect her innocent comment had on Maddie, poured a glass of sparkling water. She handed it to Maddie. "I'm not exactly sure, but I think it was at some chocolate fest."

The effervescence soothed the lump stuck in Maddie's throat. She couldn't lie and say she never went to chocolate events. After all, she had run into Brad at such a venue. Over her shoulder she noticed him leaning against the counter. With his arms crossed he listened intently to their conversation.

"I've got to go." Maddie could feel anxiety creeping under her skin. Unsure if the glimmer of recognition in the pastry chef's eyes disturbed her more than actually walking into the kitchen, Maddie backed away. The space between the counters was narrow, and once again she found herself leaning against Brad.

What was happening? Why couldn't she just get away from him?

And if she wasn't close enough . . . Nona squeezed behind her with a tray full of cannoli shells, making it impossible for Maddie to escape.

Maddie stiffened and looked apologetically over her shoulder. Brad didn't mind at all. His hands on her waist, strong and caressing, helped steady her.

The tingling in the pit of her stomach had nothing to do with the wonderful kitchen smells reminding her she was hungry. Her closeness to Brad was becoming dangerous. A handsome man with a gentle concern for everyone, he was nothing like the man she had vowed to seek revenge on.

"I really must go." Maddie inched away.

"Nonsense. You'll help make some cannolis." Nona settled her tray on the counter. "No one ever turns down an invitation to make my cannolis. Sit and watch the girls, they're good at this."

Maddie's hands itched to get hold of the pastry bag filled with the creamy filling, but she couldn't do it— even if she could fill more shells than anyone here. And that was what she was afraid of, being discovered for who she really was, an ex-pastry chef who had made a soap powder torta.

"Sit," Nona insisted. It was more an order than a request. She gestured to a vacant barstool next to the twins.

Maddie obeyed. How could you say no to a lady whose face looked like it belonged on a jar of marinara sauce?

"You know how to use a pastry bag?" Nona shoved a bag into Maddie's hand. "Watch Sophia and Emily, they'll show you how it's done." She nodded in Brad's direction. "Even he can fill a cannoli."

Maddie felt like everyone watched and waited for her to make a move. She glanced at Lily from the corner of her eye. The spiky-haired chef watched Maddie too. Feigning ignorance, Maddie pretended to watch the girls fill the empty shells, but the familiar sights and smells distracted her.

Tony went back to work supervising his sous chef. He inspected a pile of mushrooms, helped clean the counter, and handed the young man several bags of carrots. Everyone had to start somewhere. You didn't just become a top chef.

Maddie remembered her mentor, an easily excited French pastry chef. It had been under his supervision that she had created her famous torta di chocolate and moved up in the ranks.

Her sense of smell was assaulted by the scent of warm brownies. She let her memories slip away and followed her nose to the oven where Lily was removing a tray.

"Do I smell cherry mixed with chocolate?" Maddie asked.

"Yes." Lily looked up. "We serve them with cherry gelato, but not tonight." She showed Maddie the tray. "They're ruined." With all the commotion, Lily had misjudged the baking time and the brownies were a bit underdone. "I can't rebake them." She carried the tray toward the trash.

"Wait." Maddie felt responsible for the state of the brownies. Her arrival had caused a bit of a ruckus when she hesitated at the door. She knew how to fix it, how to turn them from a mistake to a delightful dessert. Should she offer a suggestion?

From the corner of her eye, Lily watched Maddie study the underdone brownies. "Any ideas?"

The way Lily scrutinized Maddie made her wish she had never agreed to meet Brad this morning. Maddie looked around the kitchen, surveying the organized shelves of pots and baking pans. She had a solution. It was risky and might alert someone to her skill. If Lily realized Maddie's identity it was best to put a safe distance between her and Brad. She walked toward the oven. "Don't throw them away."

Lily stopped, turned to Maddie, and whispered, "I've figured out who you are—the soap powder torta chef." With the half-baked brownies in her mitted hands she nodded in Brad's direction and giggled. "He has no clue, right?"

Maddie stifled her moan. On a reality TV show this scene would be good for the ratings: undercooked brownies, a cute little pastry chef, and a clueless handsome man. In real life, especially Maddie's reality, nothing about this held even a hint of humor. Silently, her eyes pleaded with Lily not to reveal her identity.

"Don't worry. Your secret is safe with me. Your

chocolate torta was the best in the city. I remember the year you won first prize at the fest."

"Were you a competitor?" Maddie asked.

"No. My family was one of the sponsors."

"Your family. What did you say your name was?" Companies sponsoring events like the New York Chocolate Fest were usually big names in the industry.

"Lily Peradou."

"Wow, a Peradou. You're like chocolate royalty." Maddie smiled. It was easy to like Lily. Maddie believed she would keep her secret, even in enemy territory. "What are you doing here?"

"I'm the youngest of my siblings. I'll never inherit the throne." Lily released a long sigh. "It's okay. I don't enjoy being stuck in an office. My brothers are much more logical than I am."

"Logical thinkers usually lack creativity. Maybe you'll find the balance." Maddie wasn't going to judge Lily's creative side because of her brownie mishap.

"Do you have that balance?" Lily asked.

Maddie shook her head. She couldn't find the words to confess that she'd never had a logical side. Perhaps if she did she might have found a way out of this mess. And now her creative muse was gone as well.

"I have to tell you I was a frequent customer at Zest until you . . ."

"Until I was fired," Maddie whispered, aware that Brad, although busy with his girls, was only feet away. There was something therapeutic in actually saying out loud what she had tried to suppress for months. Geraldine would be impressed.

"You probably realize Brad's not a bad guy. His review was unfair. You need to prove him wrong."

"Prove him wrong?" There was nothing she would have liked better, but how? Maddie's runaway muse had taken all her confidence away too.

"Yes. Make him eat his words." Lily smiled. "The time will come. Don't worry."

Maddie refrained from hugging her new ally. It felt good to have someone share her secret. In return for Lily's sympathetic words Maddie offered a suggestion to save her brownies. "Try baking your brownies into a different shape. They'll only need a few more minutes in the oven if you transfer them to a different pan."

Following Maddie's gaze in the direction of a pile of small round spring pans, Lily immediately understood her intention.

"Wow, great idea." She gathered the pans and pressed the half-baked brownies into the bottoms of six of them. Pleased with the rescue plan, she slid the half dozen spring pans into the oven.

While they waited for the cakes to bake, Maddie learned how Lily had come to work at Nona's. Lily, it turned out, had a knack for sculpting in chocolate and preferred to develop her talent here, in the trenches, instead of sitting behind the scenes at corporate headquarters. No doubt she would one day find the balance needed to run the Peradou empire.

"You're very talented," Maddie said. She dared to imagine one of Lily's whimsical carvings on top of one of her cakes. That's when the idea came to her. "A mile-high brownie cake with a chocolate spoon resting on top," she exclaimed out loud, attracting everyone's attention, especially Brad's. Oh, no, now she had gotten herself into a gooey mess she doubted she would be able to get out of.

"Yes." Lily clapped her hands together. "We'll make a brownie layer cake."

"With cannoli filling?" The twins were at Maddie's side and Brad stood behind them.

Cautiously, Maddie glanced in their direction. "I think that would work nicely."

"At least six layers high," Lily said. "A glaze dripping down the side would be the perfect topping."

"Not too sugary sweet; it would kill the cake." Maddie's words came out so fast she had no time to regret what she had just said.

Nona joined the group and handed Lily a pastry bag. "Go ahead, try it. If it works we'll put it on the menu."

Lily took the bag and handed it to Maddie. "You do it. The cake is your idea." She leaned close and whispered, "We'll call it Maddie's Resurrection."

With open palms, Maddie shied away. She couldn't add the creamy center, not with Brad Angelo and his entire family watching. But she wasn't getting out of this so easily. Encouraging words and praise for her cake save echoed around the kitchen.

Still afraid of her identity being discovered, Maddie took a breath before responding. She inhaled the fragrant scent of citron zest mixed into the filling. The scent had a strange calming effect, as if it were speaking to her, encouraging her to move forward without fear. She reached for the bag and applied the white cream to the first layer.

Over her shoulder, Brad examined her work. His breath on her neck made her entire body tingle with excitement. Difficult as it was, she continued to work. Concentrating on her creation, she pretended he wasn't there. The next five layers stacked with ease until she'd completed a magnificent mile-high brownie cake.

"Ta da!" With a professional flare, Maddie swirled the plate for everyone to see.

Applause came from Uncle Tony. The looks of gratitude from her appreciative audience sent her lost spirit soaring. Drifting somewhere on a creamy cloud, she was taken completely off guard when Brad placed his hands on her shoulders and twirled her around. They stood face to face for one long silent moment. His approval was obvious, but the smoldering look she saw in his eyes startled her.

"You're amazing," he said. "This has to be more than just a hobby for you."

"Just a hobby." She shrugged, hoping he believed her. "I like playing around with chocolate."

"I'm beginning to doubt that." He looked serious for a moment, then added, "I have a challenge for you."

Maddie felt an uneasy curiosity urging her to hear what he had to say.

"I challenge you to a cannoli-filling contest." His invitation was a passionate challenge, hard to resist. "I'd bet you fill them like a professional."

Despite the anxiety running through her, she found herself reacting to his enthusiasm. She had stepped into Nona's kitchen and found herself transformed to her favorite place, a working kitchen full of devoted staff. The crew heard Brad throw down the gauntlet and waited for her to accept the challenge.

"Are you sure you're up to this?" Maddie's heart had settled down to an even beat.

"I'm fully recovered from my visit to the ER, if that's what you're referring to."

"Good because I'm going to whip the filling out of your cannolis." Maddie stepped up to the counter. Lily gave her a thumbs-up and took her place next to Maddie. The twins and Nona lined up a row of empty shells.

This was only a small way to right the wrong done to her. Maddie would show him her true talent and he wouldn't even suspect what she was doing. The pastry bag felt so right in her hands, she no longer wanted to fake her amateur status. She started to fill one cannoli after another.

Out of the corner of her eye she watched Brad fill his shells. She hated to admit he appeared up to the challenge. But when he looked up, directly at her, his hand slipped. A line of filling covered the counter.

The twins giggled. "Go, Miss Maddie! Go, Miss Maddie."

"Unfair. My own blood is turning against me." Brad swirled his finger in the filling. He put a dab on the tips of the twins' noses. "That's for siding with the opposition."

He reached across the counter, aiming for Maddie. He stopped and changed his tactics. "Want a taste?"

"I'm not so easily distracted," she lied. The playful banter was affecting her. With the tip of her tongue she licked the filling off his finger. Their eyes met across the counter and neither of them moved. Her heart raced and heat soared through her body, warming her cheeks. *Now who was being unfair?*

Brad found his voice first. "Don't think my little setback will give you an advantage." His eyes sparkled with a playful twinkle.

Maddie no longer cared if she beat Brad or not; she was having too much fun. Brad seemed to have slowed down. He watched her work with intent interest. By the time the filling was gone, Maddie had filled two dozen cannolis to Brad's one dozen.

Brad picked up one of her stuffed cannolis. He examined her work and smiled. This insignificant victory made her feel good, but a remnant of revenge still lingered. When the truth did come out, Brad Angelo would eat his words on top of a chocolate torta sans soap.

On her way out, Maddie was more at ease and took the opportunity to look around the dining room. Italian scenes covered the walls and red-and-white-checked tablecloths covered the tables.

Brad walked ahead, following the girls outside. Uncle Tony, Nona, and Lily walked beside Maddie.

"I bet not much has changed since you first opened," Maddie said.

Tony offered a brief history of the place. "The restaurant has been in this neighborhood for several decades. Nona opened the place and did all the cooking back then. She still cooks for some of her old customers."

"A place like this must have lots of regular customers." She couldn't contain her curiosity. Successful restaurants were the envy and dream of every chef. "Is business still good?"

"Not what it was in its heyday." Tony shrugged. "We do okay."

"Nona's cannolis are pretty famous." Maddie made sure Brad was out of hearing and asked, "Have you ever thought of adding a pastry bar?" She looked at Lily. "You have a talented pastry chef in your kitchen."

"With a little redesigning that might work." Tony glanced around the restaurant as if seeing it for the first time. He turned his attention back to Maddie. "How do you know so much about the business?"

Unsure how to answer, she said, "I have some friends who own a cupcake shop. They put in some outside seating and added a coffee bar. The additions and some free publicity were a big boost to their business."

"Oh." Tony didn't sound convinced.

"You come back and we'll talk about all this." Nona sounded interested. Maddie wasn't sure if she wanted to hear more about Maddie's idea or about Maddie.

Chapter Six

A week had passed since the night at Nona's and the twins were still talking about it. Brad didn't mind because he couldn't remember when he had had so much fun. It was strange having two know-it-all seven-year-olds throw around a topic that you felt uncomfortable discussing. If he was trying to get information about their baking teacher without prying too much, they were the perfect source.

With his hands on the steering wheel, Brad waited for the crossing guard to give him the go-ahead. He couldn't get this drop-off line thing down the way some of the other parents had. He always came too late to be up front. The same SUVs and minivans always seemed to be ahead of him for drop-off as well as pickup. What did they do—sleep here?

In the back of his BMW the twins usually fidgeted and complained. They were always eager to join their classmates and socialize before the bell rang. Today, however, they were too engrossed in reviewing the details of their evening at Nona's to notice.

"Miss Maddie must have filled a gazillion cannolis." Sophia wiggled back and forth on her booster seat to emphasize how fast the cannolis were filled.

"Much faster than you did, Dad," Emily added.

"Wow, a gazillion. It seemed like only a couple dozen to me." Brad was not just playing along with the girls. He wondered about Miss Maddie's constantly surfacing talents and why they were such a big secret. "I wonder where she learned to do that."

"Cannoli school, I think," Emily stated, as if it were obvious.

Emily wasn't so far off. There was no question in his mind that Miss Maddie had some kind of formal training. A person didn't continue to show up at chocolate events by chance. And her knowledge of spices and chocolate blends was definitely greater than that of the average chocolate lover. He doubted her knowledge stemmed from just an interest in the sensual confection. He wouldn't be surprised if she had spent time studying the subject.

For a reason he couldn't quite understand, he felt his presence and questions disturbed her. She had seemed flustered whenever she noticed him paying close attention.

"You know, Dad, you should ask Miss Maddie out on a date." That surprise comment came from Sophia, the more aloof of the twins. Ever since his divorce he had noticed her lack of interest in activities. She mostly followed her sister's lead.

"Where would you suggest I take her?"

"You could go to Nona's and have pizza or spaghetti."

"I'll think about it." His meddling grandmother's restaurant was the last place he would bring Maddie—if he did ask her out and if she accepted.

Fortunately, the conversation ended. The crossing guard tapped the front of the BMW with her obtrusive sign and waved him forward. "Move up, move up! You're holding up the line!" she shouted.

"What line?" Brad said out loud to no one in particular. In the rearview mirror he saw only two cars behind him. At least he wasn't the last one today.

The girls knew the routine, which Brad had only recently learned. They gathered their backpacks, stepped out of the car, and waved good-bye.

Just as he was about to pull away from the curb, the vehicle behind him pulled in front of his car. Brad gave an exasperated sigh and wondered which single mom would step out of the monster vehicle and invite him to spend the morning drinking lattes.

Within seconds, a tall blond pounded on his window. "Brad, Brad, is that you?" Recently divorced, Cathy Coffee, Tea, or Me stood alongside the driver's window.

"Hi, Cathy." He rolled down the window. Cathy might understand better than he did the carpool rules and how to mother, but Brad didn't envy any single parent struggling to balance adult normalcy and parenting. He couldn't help but wonder what was on her agenda today—coffee or a playdate?

"I read your first piece on the cooking class your girls are enrolled in." She folded her elbows on the open window and leaned over, giving him a view of her cleavage and more. "Do you think there's still an opening for my Sasha? We could carpool."

Okay, he looked. After all, he wasn't dead, just uninterested. "I'll check and get back to you." Brad had no idea if the class was filled or not. She was the last person he wanted showing up at class. He worried that Maddie might get the wrong idea.

The twins were not the only ones with a growing affection for their cooking instructor. He liked Maddie even though he didn't know much about her. She had a dressed-down style that she wore with grace. No high-fashion antics for this lady. Brad had been attracted to her the moment he saw her.

She had been full of surprises from the time of their first encounter. After the events at Nona's, Brad could add Miss Maddie's skill with a pastry bag to the growing list of her talents. He had been a little taken aback when her final cannoli count was double his.

"How about taking the girls out for pizza tonight?" Cathy reached in and touched his shoulder. "We could stop for dessert at the little chocolate shop you wrote about."

"Baking class tonight." He shrugged apologetically.

"Don't forget. You *will* try to get Sasha into the class."

"You got it." He gave her a thumbs-up and pushed her request to a place in his mind where he would never think about it again. She was still standing on the curb, waving, as he pulled away.

Brad walked into his home office. The girls had been using his computer paper again. Crayon drawings covered the walls. Stick figures resembling people and long skinny tubes he assumed were cannolis covered the pages. He smiled, refilled the printer tray, turned on his computer, and prepared to work.

A two-day-old pile of mail distracted him. He moved fast, wanting to get the task completed so he could get to work. He quickly filed the bills and shredded the junk mail. A fancy invitation at the bottom of the pile caught his attention. The address didn't look familiar. He searched for something to open the envelope. A plastic knife would have to do.

Neil Enzo, a popular New York chef, announced the opening of another new restaurant.

"Nice invitation." He turned it over in his hand, admiring the classy style. Neil tended to be a bit flamboyant, but this invitation showed no sign of his famous exuberance. Brad wondered what all this meant.

One night at an Enzo party and Brad would have a plethora of information to keep his readers entertained for weeks. Of course he'd attend. He checked off the appropriate box. At the "plus one," he hesitated.

Brad had gone solo to events since his divorce. This

was an event he couldn't afford to miss. Bringing a date might not be such a bad idea. But no matter what the divorced moms at the girl's school thought, Brad wasn't sure if he was ready to date.

He had the girls to think about. If he could find someone agreeable to both him and the twins, he might take a shot.

He glanced at the girls' drawings. The curly-haired stick figure, Maddie, the gazillion cannoli-stuffer, immediately came to mind. He owed her for helping him out the other day, and the twins liked her. A ticket to an Enzo party would be a nice way to say thank you.

Would the lady who acted like she was in some kind of chocolate protection program want to be around so many people? There was only one way to find out. He picked up the phone and dialed the Chocolate Boutique.

"Chocolate Boutique," Chloe Behar answered.

Maddie would be in later. Brad preferred to call her now, before he lost his nerve. Without any coaxing or turning on the charm, Brad asked for Maddie's cell number. On the other end, Chloe seemed more than willing to help him get in touch with her friend.

"That was easy," he said as he dialed Maddie and waited for her to pick up.

A sleepy voice on the other end answered, "Hello?"

Brad glanced at his watch. It was already eight o'clock. Okay, so not everyone had kids to drive to school. He pictured her stretching, a sleepy yawn, and her mop of curls tossed across her pillow. He smiled, his thoughts turning away from his reason for calling.

"Uh, Maddie? Hi, This is Brad, Brad Angelo. Did I wake you?"

"Kind of." She yawned.

He exhaled and refocused. "I don't know if you're interested, but I've been invited . . ." He cleared his throat. He was so out of touch with this dating thing. "I'm sure you've heard of the chef Neil Enzo."

"Neil Enzo." Maddie suddenly seemed very awake. "You've been invited to a Neil Enzo party?"

"Um, yes. Want to go?" For an articulate reporter, Brad was having a hard time finding the right words. He wiped his forehead and reminded himself he was doing this for Sophia.

An uncomfortable silence followed.

"Can I let you know?" Her voice went from intrigued to cautious.

"Oh, okay. Think about it? I don't have to respond for a few days." He had the impression she was trying hard not to like him but wasn't succeeding.

"I'll consider it." She hadn't jumped at his offer, but she hadn't refused either. "Are you coming to my class this evening?" Maddie asked.

"Yes, I have to drop off the girls. I'll bring the invitation." Brad was not easily impressed, but this invitation had grabbed his attention. It had given him a reason to call Maddie. He hoped the sight of the invitation would dazzle her into accepting.

"Does it smell like chocolate?" Maddie asked. "I've heard that Neil likes to stimulate all the senses with his invites."

"No." Brad took a sniff. "It smells like paper to me." There was nothing stimulating about the scent of the invitation, but the sleepy voice on the other end of the receiver had aroused his senses better than his morning coffee. He didn't want to hang up just yet. "By the way, what's on the menu tonight?" If she planned to cover wood with chocolate Brad would be at her class.

"Nothing as exciting as eating chocolate at a Neil Enzo party," Maddie said, then added, "Plain, old-fashioned chocolate chip cookies are the subject tonight."

"I doubt there'll be anything plain about your cookies."

"What do you mean?" She seemed anxious.

"Your hidden culinary skills seem to appear out of nowhere."

"I have a natural gift, I suppose."

"You've got more than a gift. You've got a real flair for working with chocolate." Suppressing his curiosity was becoming more and more difficult. There were a million questions he wanted to ask her, not for his article, but to satisfy his need to know more about her. Why couldn't she be honest with him?

"It's nothing special, just your average interest in anything chocolate."

Much more than average. Brad kept his thoughts to himself. Sometimes she acted like some kind of Mata

Hari, alluding to a secret and pulling away when he got too close. "I'll see you this evening."

"See you later." Maddie hung up.

Yes, Maddie Higgins would be the perfect date for the grand opening of a restaurant owned by a colorful chef like Neil Enzo. Wacky as he was, Neil loved chocolate, and Maddie would love Neil's flare for the enticing treat.

There was always the chance she would refuse, Brad pushed the thought from his mind.

Chapter Seven

Maddie paced back and forth in the empty classroom. Except for Chloe, who had donated the chocolate
for tonight's cookies, no one had arrived yet.

Chloe handed her Brad's article about the Chocolate
Boutique. "Read it before you pass judgment," Chloe
insisted.

Brad's byline photo smiled at Maddie. "I can't." She
looked away, afraid the article would bring back those
horrid images. It had been a while since she had experienced the visual memory of Brad choking. Geraldine
attributed it to actually coming face-to-face with him.
Her imagination no longer controlled her thoughts.

"Believe me, he didn't say anything bad or mention
you by name," Chloe reassured her.

"You're sure he didn't trash your shop?" Maddie
glanced at the article. "I can't," she said again, and tossed
the paper on the counter.

Chloe retrieved it and gave her a brief synopsis. "He

liked the shop and never mentioned you or his trip to the emergency room."

"He didn't?" Maddie couldn't hide the doubt from her voice. "Maybe it's hidden between the lines."

"No. He didn't say one bad thing about the entire experience. As a matter of fact, his brief mention of the Mayan bowls has set off a wave of calls from groups and teachers interested in visiting the shop."

"You can thank him for the plug when he gets here."

"When will that be?"

Maddie glanced at her watch. "Any minute." Some of her students were gathering in the hallway.

Maddie was dying to share the news with someone that she had been invited to attend the grand opening of Neil Enzo's new restaurant. She fiddled with the wrappers of the chocolate bars Chloe had donated to the class.

"Why are you so nervous?" Chloe gave her a curious glance. "Is there something you want to tell me?"

"Brad invited me to the grand opening of Neil Enzo's new place," Maddie blurted. "I can't show up at Neil's party. Not with the man who ruined my career." From the corner of her eye she looked at Chloe, hoping she would offer a suggestion.

"Wow, Neil Enzo." Chloe grabbed Maddie's hands. "How can you refuse an invitation like that? His parties are a chocolate lover's dream."

"Sure, a chocolate lover's dream, but a nightmare for Neil's old friend, the soap powder chef."

"Hmm. You do have a point." Chloe nodded in agreement. "I'm sure Neil would be glad to see you, though. Has he been in touch since the"—Chloe cleared her throat—"incident?"

"You were the only one I spoke to for weeks." Maddie fidgeted with a cookie cutter. "Neil knows everyone in the business. How will I explain showing up with the man who stole my muse?"

"There's only one thing for you to do." Chloe shrugged. "You'll just have to tell Brad who you are so you won't have to worry about someone breaking the news at the party."

"Are you nuts?"

"No. Not as crazy as you are if you're willing to miss one of Neil's parties because of a little misunderstanding."

"A little misunderstanding?" Maddie needed more time to erase the memory. She wasn't ready for this. She still wanted to dislike Brad. "Whose side are you on?"

"Yours. It's time he learned your little secret. You should put the incident behind you and go with him to the party."

"Do I have to do both?" Maddie groaned. "Can't I just go to the party?"

"Do you want to take the chance?" Chloe threw the paper on the table and poked her finger at Brad's article. "He's not so bad. Look at the nice story he wrote about my shop."

"You were just lucky." Maddie rolled her eyes. "Maybe he was in a good mood when he wrote this piece."

"Have you ever seen him grumpy?" Chloe asked.

Maddie thought for a moment. "No, never. That's the problem, he's always so nice to me." How could she hold a grudge against a man who teased her with his smile? "Now I know why mothers always tell you to tell the truth."

"You should have told him who you were the night you saw him at the book signing."

"I couldn't." Maddie shook her head. "I despised Brad Angelo the food writer."

"It's obvious he likes you," Chloe said. "If he didn't, he wouldn't have invited you to the party."

Maddie blushed. She knew her friend was right. Brad Angelo was not the type to invite just anyone to such an important event.

"How do you feel about him, now?" Chloe asked.

"How can I like him? I'm supposed to hate him."

"But you do have feelings for him." Chloe giggled.

"Not always positive. You're beginning to sound just like Geraldine." Maddie turned and walked away. Her students were filing into the room.

The twins came running over to her. "Hi, Miss Maddie. Daddy's not coming. Nona drove us here."

"Oh." Maddie felt relief mixed with disappointment. Brad had said he would be here, and she wouldn't admit, even to Chloe, that she was a bit disappointed. On the other hand, she wouldn't have to make any decisions this evening.

But she was curious and asked, "Where's your dad?"

The girls shrugged. Nona came up behind them. "A rival magazine invited him to join a food tasting. He sends his apologies."

"No problem. He's not actually registered as a student." Maddie wondered how he would write the next article in his series if he didn't observe her class. "Let's get started." She clapped her hands to get everyone's attention.

Chloe was not the only one excited about Brad's literary skills. The class was buzzing with talk about his first article on the generational baking class. Several of the students had been mentioned by name. They were unable to contain their excitement, forcing Maddie to read the piece.

Maddie had avoided that article too. She didn't want to read anything written by Brad Angelo.

Sadie Katz shoved the paper in her face, leaving her with little choice.

"Go on, read it." Sadie beamed proudly and pointed to the line describing her ability to use a whisk like a professional.

Maddie forced a smile. Even though the words were no more than a jumble, she looked at the headline. Maddie scanned the page, anxious that she might find her name in the article too.

Nothing. Not even a reference to the teacher. He had kept his word.

Okay, so he wasn't such a cad. Brad Angelo had actually written a very entertaining piece describing the goals of the community center through the eyes of the students. Too bad he wasn't going to be here tonight.

Her class was anxious to start. "There are no limits to your creativity," Maddie explained. She showed them how to mix and roll the cookie dough. They used an assortment of Chloe's broken chocolate bars as chips.

Nona turned out to be the star of the evening, suggesting unusual twists on the standard chocolate chip cookie. During the class break Nona approached Maddie about her suggestion for a dessert bar. Lily had been very receptive, and suggested the restaurant do a dessert-tasting event as a market test. Maddie agreed the event was a great idea.

When the class resumed, Maddie gladly relinquished her spot to Nona. She sat back contemplating her future. Chloe sat down next to her.

"I overheard your conversation with Nona. Do you think she knows your true connection to her grandson?"

"Lily knows. I wouldn't be surprised if she told her boss."

"So." Chloe gave her a sideways glance. "Have you decided? Are you going to tell him the truth?"

"Maybe I should, while he still has a good feeling about me," Maddie said. How could she lie to such a man? His integrity made her deceit feel like she was playing a dirty trick. "But not tonight."

She thought back to the evening at Nona's. His interest in her had been obvious. How easy it would be to slip into his life. But such an attraction could be danger. She had decided then that it would be best if their relationship did not involve a romantic interest. After all, when the classes ended she would never see him again.

She had plans.

"I'm thinking about taking a trip when my contract ends," Maddie confessed. "Remember how we always wanted to stay in Europe after graduating from the École du Chocolat?"

Chloe nodded and gave her a curious look. "Can you afford it?"

"With the money I saved and my unemployment checks I could turn the trip into a new chocolate venture." Maddie watched the twins mix a batch of lemon-pepper chips into the batter. She had discovered how to tell them apart. Sophia, the quieter twin, was left-handed and Emily right-handed. She would miss the girls.

"You know I thought of doing the same thing a few years ago." Chloe patted her big round belly. "Where would you live? What would you do?"

"Maybe I'll go to Belgium or Denmark. Did you know that the Danes think of chocolate as a vegetable? It comes from the cocoa bean and beans are a vegetable. You gotta love people who put chocolate into a food group. Those are my kind of people."

Chloe laughed, but looked sad. "You're serious, aren't you?"

"It's just a thought. I have a friend in Belgium. She rents a small apartment for about five hundred euro a month. I could live with her awhile. I'm sure I could get a job selling chocolate."

"Selling chocolate." Chloe looked disappointed. "What a waste of your talent."

"What talent? I haven't been able to mix two ingredients together for fear of the outcome." Maddie had not shared her experience in Nona's kitchen with her friend. But even then, she had only made suggestions and worked with a filling that had been made by someone else.

A loud clank interrupted the conversation. Sophia had insisted on carrying a tray of cookies to the oven and tripped. Several dozen doughy mounds of unbaked cookies stuck to the floor. Sophia stood over them. Big tears rolled down her cheeks.

Maddie rushed over and put her arm around the child. There was no way to salvage the cookies. While Nona cleaned up the mess, Maddie took Sophia back to the table. Most of Chloe's chips had been used, leaving them with little to work with.

"I've got an idea," Maddie whispered in Sophia's ear. "We'll bake the biggest cookie and sprinkle it with all the different-flavored slivers of chocolate."

"The biggest." Sophia stopped crying and looked up at Maddie as if she were a chocolate goddess.

While the rest of the class sampled their baked treats, Maddie and Sophia waited for their giant cookie to bake. The class had made a delicious assortment of chocolate chip cookies. They were so good that Chloe offered to bring more broken chocolate bars if the class would bake them into cookies. She offered to box them and sell the cookies as a fundraiser for the center.

Maddie wished Brad were here to experience her students' excitement. This would be good material for his series and a big plug for the center.

The frosting on the evening was Sophia's giant cookie. Eight inches in diameter and covered with melted chocolate, it was a pretty impressive sight.

"That's the biggest cookie I've ever seen," Nona complimented Sophia.

Everyone rushed over for a taste.

When the last crumb was gone and the utensils cleaned and put away for the next class, Maddie dismissed the group. Chloe ran off to meet her husband, Ethan, for dinner. Nona left with the girls.

Maddie stood alone in the big empty room. For the first time in a long time she felt pride in the work she was doing. She shut off the lights and left the room.

At the end of the corridor she saw a man. At first she thought it might be the night janitor.

He leaned against the wall and watched her approach. Closer up there was no mistaking Brad Angelo for the janitor. Maddie hesitated a moment, inhaling the clean masculine scent of his homemade soap. A few steps closer and she noticed the flicker of the overhead lights accentuating his steel-gray eyes. How had his evening been? Who was invited to the event? Could they concentrate on food when someone who looked so striking in a tux sat across the table?

"Hi." His greeting echoed in the empty hallway. "I ran into my grandmother and the girls on my way in."

Maddie regained her composure. Why hadn't he just taken the girls and left? What was he doing here?

"The class is over," she said. "I wish I had some samples for you to taste. Chloe took the few leftover cookies back to her shop."

"So I've heard. The girls were all excited. They told me how you came to the rescue and saved the day."

"You know how it is with chocolate chip cookies. They're always a hit with everyone," she answered matter-of-factly.

"That's not what I heard." He stepped closer. "I heard you made a gigantic cookie for Sophia." There was no mistaking the gratitude in his voice. "She's definitely my more sensitive twin. Thanks for making her feel so special."

"They're great kids. You've done a good job." Maddie looked up at him and wondered if he ever felt the strain of being a single parent.

"Want to have a cup of coffee and tell me what I missed?" His eyes were soft and questioning, and for some unknown reason, had the power to command her to agree to his request.

She tried to convince herself the flutter in the pit of her stomach was because she wanted to share the excitement of the evening and had nothing to do with his charming smile.

Her thoughts about Belgium slipped to the back burner.

Chapter Eight

Y ou can't possibly be hungry after the food tasting."
Maddie stared across the chrome-plated table and watched
Brad scoop a forkful of cherry pie into his mouth.

"I can't come into this diner and not order their cherry
pie." He pushed the plate across the table. "You're right,
though. I had one dessert too many this evening. Want
to taste the pie?"

"I'll take your word for it." Maddie held up an open
palm. "I'm sure it's delicious, but I'll pass."

The diner had been a good choice. No one looked
twice when Brad in his custom tuxedo and Maddie in
last season's jeans and a secondhand T-shirt slipped into
a corner booth. Maddie, however, could not take her eyes
off him. It had nothing to do with how nice he looked in
his tux. She sat there contemplating his affection for his
girls and his strong ties to his family.

He removed his tie and opened the top button of his
shirt, revealing a tuft of chest hair.

With his hands clasped behind his head, he leaned

back against the red vinyl seat, turned his smile up a notch, and said, "Tell me about your evening."

"You already know we made a giant cookie. Tell me about the event you went to." Never in this lifetime would Maddie ever have imagined that she and Brad Angelo would be sitting across a table from one another, smiling and joking like old friends.

"The event was made up of mostly local chefs with new dishes they're considering adding to their menus."

"Anything exciting?" Maddie wanted to hear what other people were creating.

"You can read about it in my column tomorrow." He looked at her intently. "I'd rather discuss your class."

This would be the perfect opportunity to tell him who she was, confess that she was his soap powder torta chef. Would the information drastically change his mind about her? Her heart sunk at the thought that it would.

Maddie fidgeted with her napkin. She wanted to tell him all about her class, but feared her enthusiasm would lead to more questions she didn't want to answer. She'd give him just enough information for his article and make sure he plugged the center. Maybe later she would find the right place to slip in the truth. "What did the girls tell you?"

"I got a jumbled story on my way in. Something about broken chocolate bars with pepper and lemon flavoring and your giant cookie." His face lit up when he spoke about his daughters.

"That kind of sums up the class. Chloe donated some

broken chocolate bars and I suggested we use them as flavored chips for our cookies."

"And Sophia's giant cookie?" He continued to question her, not satisfied with her answer. "You appear to have another save under your belt. First Lily's brownies and now Sophia's cookie."

"Wow. You got lots of information in a short time."

"The twins can talk fast, especially when they're excited." He paused, looking at her with caution before adding his own opinion. "Your class is more stimulating than I imagined it would be."

"Thanks." Feeling a bit awkward, Maddie wiggled back in her seat. Did he think she was as exciting as her class?

"I have to confess that I thought an old lady from the neighborhood would be the teacher." Placing his folded elbows on the table, he leaned forward.

"Sorry to disappoint you."

"I have never been less disappointed." His voice deepened and something on the edge of seduction hovered in the tone. "I know you've worked with chocolate before, but are you sure you never baked professionally?"

"The truth is . . ." How desperately Maddie wanted to tell him the truth and move on, whatever the consequences. Her mouth felt dry.

The waitress filled Maddie's coffee cup. She watched the steam rise over the rim while she waited for her beverage to cool. The few seconds it took gave her time to reconsider her almost-confession. She decided against it. "I took some courses."

Another opportunity to tell the truth had melted away. Maddie hadn't been able to find the words.

"You must have had some great instructors."

"A few." Actually they had been quite famous. Maddie fondly remembered her teachers at the École du Chocolat. She had been one of their best students. What would they say about her current state of employment?

"You don't give yourself enough credit. You know how to inspire your students."

"Being creative with chocolate is not hard." Maddie shrugged. "The chocolate tells you what to do."

"That's a clever twist. Mind if I use it in my article?"

"As long as you don't quote me." If she could only be as creative as Brad in her storytelling ability, she might be able to give credibility to her reason for deceiving him. The more she thought about it, the more she realized it had been her own sorry need for revenge that kept her from disclosing her true identity. He would never know the weeks she had spent drowning her misery in ice cream while she planned how she would get back at his cruel and unfair words. Now, he sat across from her, enchanting her with his sparkling eyes and charming smile.

"No quotes, no names, no photos." He made a little X over his heart. "Don't blame me if word of your talent spreads. Lily is still talking about your mile-high brownie cake."

"The brownie recipe is Lily's and the cannoli filling is your grandmother's blend." Here they were talking about another complication in this sticky concoction she had created. "The cake is theirs to serve as they wish."

"I think they're going to name it after you and put it on the menu at Nona's. Nona and Lily mentioned presenting it at some kind of dessert night," he said, then added, "They said you gave them the idea."

"Me? What would I know about a dessert night?"

"Maybe I misunderstood." He shrugged and gave her a curious look.

Maddie took the opportunity to direct the conversation back to Lily's cake. "A menu item called *Maddie's Cannoli Cake* doesn't sound very enticing."

"Hmm. How about Maddie in the Sky?" Brad waited for a response.

Maddie smiled and met his gaze. The moment lingered and she was unsure what to do. If he only knew that she felt like she *was* floating in the sky when he looked at her so intently.

She lowered her lids and folded her hands around her coffee mug. "Doesn't sound very Italian." She took a sip. "Does it mean something?"

"I have no idea." Brad shrugged. "Sounds good. No one has to understand the meaning, just be intrigued enough to order a slice."

After a moment, Maddie nodded. Sure sounded better than soap powder torta. There was no harm in having a cake named after her or showing up at Nona's again.

"You're very quick with words."

"It pays the bills."

"Did you always write about food?"

"Hey, I'm supposed to be the one asking the questions, but if I answer one will you answer one for me?"

"Okay, only one." She wished he'd stop looking at her with such intent interest. "So how did the infamous Brad Angelo get his start?"

"Would you believe it all happened because I wanted nothing to do with the food industry?" He explained how he had spent his summers traveling through Italy with his parents in search of recipes and gadgets for the restaurant.

"That explains your slight Italian accent."

"You noticed. Most people don't."

"I've got an ear for languages." Maddie knew better than to confess that was not the only thing she had noticed about him. She loved the way his eyes brightened when his daughters walked into a room and the way he spoke with his hands when he wanted to make a point. "Visiting Italy must have been exciting."

"The traveling was, but everything revolved around food and more food."

"And here you are with a popular syndicated column, all about food." She raised a brow and asked, "What happened to make you change your mind?"

"I met a chef who had traveled around the world but came back to New York to open a neighborhood restaurant. While I was building a reputation as a food writer

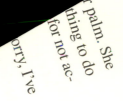

t. One day I came home and the dog walker." Maddie threw d part is, he took the dog, and, espresso machine."

?" Brad asked.

ve a chocolate Lab?"

expected any other kind."

it out part of her story. A few days later, e dog, but an unexpected phone call eased esso machine were no longer important.

s five-star restaurant.

ef. Maddie would be drinking her espresso at afe to assume there are no men in your life at the The owner of Zest offered her a position as ery safe." Maddie nodded. She watched him spear at?"

remaining cherries on the plate in front of him. Surisingly, thinking about her past life didn't leave her eeling sad.

"Then you have no reason not to go with me to Neil Enzo's party." He removed the invitation from his pocket and handed it to her.

I worked for him. The world came thr...
of his restaurant. I started writing ab...
diners and what they ate. What better...
life than to write about what people are ...

Brad had given her more than she expecte...
brief sentences he had given her a look into his p...
sensitivity and intuitiveness. She hoped he didn't exp...
the same.

"My turn." His smile held a blend of curiosity mixed
with an uncertain affection.

Waiting for the inevitable, Maddie fidgeted with her
spoon. She knew she was definitely sunk.

Brad studied her for a long agonizing moment before
he finally asked his question. "Any broken hearts in your
past?"

She released a long slow sigh, relieved that he wasn't
asking her about her last job.

"Was it that bad?" he asked.

"Was what bad?" She needed to refocus.

"Your last relationship?"

"No, not now when I look back."

"Then why the exasperated reaction?"

"I thought you were going to ask me what I want to
be when I grow up."

A sly smile tilted his lips. "Would you tell me?"

"No," she answered firmly. Maddie wasn't sure what
she wanted to do with her future. Working with chocolate
would always be a part of her life, but in what capacity
only time would tell.

Maddie let the heavy envelope rest on he...
didn't open the envelope. The weight had n...
with its contents. She had a very good reason...
cepting Brad's invitation.

Brad, noticing her hesitation, said, "Don't w...
already got my own espresso machine."

Brad looked into her dark chocolate chip ey...
the sexy depths that concealed some well-g...
secret. Whatever it was, it kept her at a distance. ...
put himself out there by inviting her to Enzo's bas...
recent divorce had left him gun-shy in the relatio...
department. But he was not the type to let the past a...
him. The time had come to move on.

He ran his fingers over his hair and waited for her ...
open the envelope. Covering the food event had be...
pleasant, but he would bet her class had been more fu...
He wished he could have seen the look on Sophia's fac...
when her giant cookie came out of the oven. No doubt...
row. He envied the twins, and with childlike jealousy he
wished he had been there.

Across the table, he watched her empty her coffee cup.
She was procrastinating.

Would she go? He wanted to ask her again without
appearing too eager.

"The invitation is definitely over the edge." She gin-
gerly slid the delicate paper, curled to resemble chocolate

ribbons, out of the envelope. "I can't imagine what the party will be like."

"Is that a yes?" Brad raised an eyebrow and waited for an excruciating moment before she answered.

"I guess so." She tried to sound nonchalant, but he noticed how she twisted her napkin into a spiral.

Brad never asked invasive questions. It wasn't his style. However, getting an ambiguous reply was usually the norm from someone who had something to hide or was nervous about the subject. If he were interviewing Maddie, which he wasn't, he would suspect she had a reason for holding back.

He could, if he wanted to investigate, find out more about her. Finding out information someone wanted to hide was what journalists did best.

Brad watched her and did want to know everything about Maddie, but not as a reporter doing an interview. He wanted to find out about the sassy woman who had managed to steal his heart. He could make a few calls. With all his connections in the food industry it wouldn't be hard to find out what Maddie was hiding. Why else would she be so secretive? She had denied protecting a secret recipe, claimed chocolate was her hobby, and was evasive about any formal training.

"Anything else?" the waitress asked.

"I'm good." Brad reached into his pocket for his wallet. He might be unsure about the new dating rules—if there were any—but his failed marriage had taught him that a relationship had to be based on trust. He would sit tight and wait for Maddie to reveal her secrets.

She must have a good reason for keeping her secret so closely guarded. He wasn't going to try and understand her just yet. If *I guess so* was all she could give him right now, he would take it.

"I got everything I need." And he truly did. He had a date. It would be the first date since his divorce.

"What about you?" The waitress turned toward Maddie. She stacked the empty coffee cups.

"I'm fine." Maddie's smile found its way through her uncertainty.

She had no idea how pretty she looked when she smiled. Her smile was more delicious than the cherry pie Brad found so irresistible.

ything would

s dilemma.
ll have no

utfit for
at an
sure
set.”
ests
o-
e

er Nine

ve that time had passed so quickly.
e had locked herself away brooding
se. The days and nights had dragged on

e was still missing, but time no longer stood
ight she would teach her last class.
ier today, she left Geraldine's office feeling more
ertain about the twists and turns in her life than when
e had first started seeing her happiness life coach.
Back then, she had only wanted revenge. Now that the
man she wanted to hate could make her weak-kneed with
his smile, she felt unsure if she was making the right
choice.

Maddie could have refused his invitation to the Enzo
event by making some sorry excuse. But did she really
want to turn down the invitation of the year? Luckily,
Geraldine helped her see that going to the party could be
the missing link she needed to inspire her muse to return.

Maddie was going in the right direction. If only she

could stop being so hard on herself, eve
fall into place.

Chloe had the perfect solution for Maddie
"It's the day before the Enzo party and you sti
idea what you're going to wear?"

"I have bigger issues to deal with than my o
tomorrow evening." Maddie shrugged. "Guests
Enzo event are limited to either black or white. I'm
I still have a standard black dress shoved into my clo

"So it's true. I had heard that Neil expects his gu
to dress that way so no one will overshadow the choc
late." Chloe wrinkled her nose. "A dress shoved in th
back of your closet will never do for such an event. This
could be your coming-out party."

When it came to fashion there was no putting it on
the back burner for Chloe. Maddie understood this would
be a losing battle. She tucked her pocketbook under her
arm and followed Chloe into one of her pre-pregnancy
haunts.

Finally seeing a hint of light at the end of her money
crunch, Maddie had been persuaded by her well-meaning
friend to visit a high-end thrift shop on Atlantic Avenue.

Inside the shop Chloe was greeted with hugs and well
wishes for her upcoming baby. She, however, was on
a mission and wasted no time explaining Maddie's im-
pending fashion disaster. The salesgirls immediately responded and guided them to a rack of expensive-looking
outfits.

"How's this one?" Chloe held up a shimmering black sheath. "Sexy, but sophisticated."

Maddie took a seat in an overstuffed chair. The price tag pinched her arm. She looked at it and said, "This looks more comfortable. Maybe I should buy the chair and forget about the dress."

"And what will you wear to the ball, Cinderella?"

"I won't go."

Chloe glanced at her watch. "You have eighteen hours before your date; you can't call and change your mind."

"Why not?" Maddie fingered the dress fabric. It was definitely silky and sexy. "Okay, I'll try it on." With a noncommittal shrug she followed Chloe to the dressing room.

"My connection to Neil is going to be a problem." Maddie slipped the dress over her head.

"I told you a long time ago you should have told Brad who you really are. The fact that you and Neil worked together as sous chefs would make perfect sense if Brad knew your real identity." Chloe zipped up the back.

"So, I either go or don't go." The image in the dressing room mirror overwhelmed Maddie. She swirled in circles, loving the look and feel of the dress, but not the price. "I thought you said this was a thrift shop?"

"It is. You couldn't afford this dress at the real price."

Maddie looked at the tag and winced. "I don't think I can afford it at this price."

"I'd bet some famous movie star or royalty wore it only once," Chloe said.

"I guess I deserve to treat myself." She glanced in the mirror again.

"You look stunning." Chloe clapped her hands. "You have to go if for no other reason than wearing this dress to the culinary event of the year."

Maddie ignored the tag dangling off the strap. Chloe was right. There was no excuse not to buy the dress.

Several more stops and Maddie's outfit was complete. After her whirlwind shopping spree, she was glad to be standing in front of her class. Her purchases—the black dress, new three-inch heels, and a vintage designer evening bag—were tucked away in a desk in the back of the room.

In honor of the Neil Enzo event tomorrow evening, Maddie had decided to teach her class the art of making chocolate ribbons. The class would be based on a semi-homemade recipe.

The homemade part consisted of a demonstration by Maddie on the art of chocolate stenciling. Stenciled ribbons would replace the standard paper cupcake holder.

The finished products might not look as picture-perfect as one of her friend Mike's cupcakes, but the class would be fun.

The process was time-consuming and Maddie decided to give the class a head start. They set up the supplies while she pre-cut plastic stencils. She was in the process of melting white chocolate for the fudge cakes when Brad walked in.

His compelling smile riveted her to the spot as he crossed the room.

She peeked over his shoulder, but didn't see the girls. "Where are Sophia and Emily?"

"They're home with my grandmother. Emily had a fever." Brad looked in the double boiler on the stovetop. "Hmm. White chocolate."

Maddie gave the pot a quick stir. "You should have stayed home and taken care of them." Silently she was glad he showed up. This might prove to be her best class. He would be so impressed with her skill that when she confessed and revealed their connection, he wouldn't even care that she had been deceiving him all along. "I would have filled you in tomorrow."

Who was she kidding? She didn't want to wait until tomorrow to see him.

"This is it, the last article of my series. I think my readers would like me to write about my hands-on experience. Don't worry about the girls; they're used to me working odd hours."

"It must be rough being a single parent." Maddie felt her heart squeeze for him. At times like this she wondered how he had gotten custody of the girls.

"I'm lucky to have my grandmother close by."

She nodded in agreement. She may not agree with what he wrote in his articles, but it was his job and he had to be where the story was.

He sounded enthusiastic and respectful when he asked, "What are we making this evening?"

"Stenciled cupcake holders."

"Who will I be working with?" He [...] over his chest and gave her a sly loo[...]

"The groups will be a little [...] twins." Maddie looked around the r[...] out, Sadie and Mr. Liang had lost the[...] evening. "You can pair up with me, Sadie, [...]

"Are you really giving me the choice?" H[...] "Who would you pick if you were in my positio[...]

"Mr. Liang?" She regarded him with a rheto[...] glance.

"Not my choice." He stepped closer. "I prefer the teacher."

She exhaled, trying to suppress the surge of heat his closeness provoked. "Aren't you afraid of being called the teacher's pet?" Certain that her entire class could see her turning cotton candy pink, she fanned herself with an open palm.

"I've been called far worse." He gave her an enticing look that hinted at wanting to be more than just the teacher's pet.

Those eyes could melt her to the spot. She had a class to teach and needed to turn her attention back to her chocolate ribbons. "Then you'd better earn the privilege." She shoved an apron and a spatula into his hands. "I have a video explaining the delicate process we're using to-night. Take a seat and pay close attention."

Maddie explained the objective for her class. "I want us to have fun this evening. A special thanks goes to

---

Maddie a thumbs-up. He was taking this serio[...] demonstrator spread her second layer of choco[...] clipped the ends of the chocolate-covered ste[...] a clothespin, forming a perfect circle. The co[...] stencil went into the refrigerator.

When it was completely dry, the demonstrator[...] away the thin layer of plastic to reveal a beautiful [...] cup waiting to be filled.

The class clapped.

Even Maddie was impressed with how easy the [...] onstrator ran through each step. Anxious to start, e[...] one rushed to their stations. Some of her students [...] right, while the others sighed with frustration. In spi[...] the video, she had to provide hands-on supervision, [...] plaining the somewhat complicated task of working [...] melted chocolate.

Brad turned out to be an eager student. His dexter[...] appeared a little off and his stenciling lopsided. [...] laughed at his missed attempts.

When everyone had successfully applied the first laye[...] of white chocolate, Maddie gave the class a break whil[...] she prepared the dark chocolate that would highlight th[...] white stencil. "The chocolate needs a short time to harden [...] before we apply the next layer."

The class moved out into the hallway.

Through the open door, Maddie overheard bits of their conversations. They were sad the class was ending. Her students hoped she would teach another session. She was Maddie's feelings were mixed, bittersweet.

proud of what she had accomplished. But she was sad too. This class had been just the catalyst she needed to get back on track, but her career plans did not include teaching adult education for the rest of her life. If she couldn't create wonderful desserts in a five-star restaurant, having her own pastry shop would be her second choice.

She dropped some chocolate squares into the double boiler and tuned out the chatter outside the classroom. The temperature was just right and the chocolate began to melt.

Brad did not join the group. He came up behind her, placed his hands on her hips, and watched over her shoulder. "Let me help." He reached around, closing his fingers over her mitted hand.

"You know what they say about too many cooks?" The gentle pressure of his hand upset Maddie's concentration. Her gloved fingers felt surprisingly warm, as did the rest of her body. "Pay close attention to the pot." She gave the chocolate one more stir to test its consistency. Brad could complete the task alone from this point.

Brad, however, wasn't looking at the pot. Maddie removed her oven mitt and hooked it on her apron. "Pay attention to the chocolate," she ordered, feeling a rush of heat.

Brad continued to ignore the chocolate. He looked serious, a little too serious. "You're on fire!" he shouted.

Maddie jumped back, away from the stove, before she discovered what was burning.

Brad reacted fast, reaching for her oven mitt. A small flame ignited the thumb. He tossed it on the floor, sending a wave of smoke up toward the ceiling.

Dumbfounded at first, she watched him stomp out the fire. A few seconds later, she noticed the glove was not the only thing sending up smoke signals.

Behind Brad, the chocolate pot started to burn. Little puffs of smoke escaped around the edges. Maddie reached for the handle. "Ouch!" She removed the double boiler with her bare hand. Too late, heat and smoke had already triggered the sprinkler system.

Water sprayed around them, and the fire alarm shrieked. Security and the janitor arrived. They shut off the sprinklers and ushered the students out of the building. Maddie insisted on staying to survey the damage. Brad convinced the school staff he would see that there were no further mishaps and Maddie would be safe.

Soaked to the bone, Maddie studied the stinging burn across her palm. The air around her smelled like burned chocolate. The pot of dark chocolate, now a sticky brown mess, sat full of water in the sink. The worktable had turned into a sea of runny chocolate ribbons and soggy cupcakes.

If the entire scene weren't such an ironic end to her class, she would have cried. "I don't belong here. I'm not a baking teacher, and now look what I've done."

"I don't think your class would agree with you. Did you hear what they had to say? They're sorry your class is ending." Brad took her over to the sink and ran cold water over her hand. "I've seen worse kitchen fires. Remember, I've been around restaurants since I was a kid."

"Why do you always say the right thing? I don't deserve it."

In the sewing center across the room, a full-length mirror reflected Maddie's disheveled image. Her hair resembled a mop head and her T-shirt clung to her like she was entered in a wet T-shirt contest. Even the soaked headless mannequin looked more attractive than she did.

Brad did not look the least bit bothered by her appearance. "Accidents happen." He patted her hand dry, lifted it to his lips, and pressed a kiss in her palm before adding, "You're too hard on yourself."

Her hand tingled where his lips had touched. An echo of Geraldine's similar words filled her mind. *Too hard on yourself.* She pulled away, fighting back the tears. "Don't you see it's dangerous for you to be near me?"

"Why don't you let me be the judge of that?" He smiled. "Maybe I like being in jeopardy; it adds excitement to my story."

"Which I've just ruined. What could you possibly write about now? It's my fault that there will be no class tonight and no final installment to your baking class series."

"You told me the other night that I was good with words." He raised a brow and asked, "Have you changed your mind?"

Ignoring his teasing she said, "But this is not the first time I put you in harm's way." Blinking rapidly, she added,

"Did you forget? I almost killed you with a chocolate tasting. I had to take you to the ER." Each time she had put him in danger, she found herself more involved in his life.

"Well, I'm still here. Hard as you try, I'm not going away." He raised a brow. "Do you want me to?"

"No," she whispered. "Remember the first time we met? I wanted you to disappear, but not anymore."

"You were in a bit of a hurry to get away. I thought maybe I had come on too strong."

If timing were everything, this might be the perfect opportunity to come clean. His soothing words and sympathetic eyes encouraged her to tell him her secret. It was as if some undeniable instinct told him to be her champion. The images of him choking had vanished, but her fear of harming someone with one of her desserts still left her vulnerable.

"I wasn't going to call," she said tentatively, before Brad interrupted.

"I know. I showed up here with the girls. I guess it was meant to be." He looked at her and smiled. "What can I do to convince you that we work well together?"

"Like oil and water?" She looked into his eyes, wishing for the perfect words to explain why their relationship was all wrong.

"More like sugar and spice." He cradled her face and kissed her. His lips sent a passionate message she couldn't ignore.

"I'm not as sweet as you think." If only she wasn't so attracted to him, it would be easier to walk away.

"Okay with me. I like my women on the sassy side." He brushed his lips across hers. "Yes, definitely spicy." He pulled her closer.

In that one quick motion she found herself in his arms. She fit so perfectly into the contour of his body, she didn't offer any resistance. Nestled in his arms, she caught a hint of his clean Italian soap. It was like a breath of fresh air in the soggy room.

She waited until her feet touched the ground and the sirens stopped vibrating in her head before she attempted to push away, but not very hard. "You don't really know me."

"If you're keeping something from me, I'm sure you have a good reason." Brad hadn't moved. His closeness and reassuring words did not make her feel better about her deception. "We've all got our little secrets."

"You've got secrets?" She looked up into the dark eyes that consumed her and wondered what he could be hiding.

"Doesn't everyone?" he asked.

A soft cough at the door informed them they were no longer alone. The fire department had arrived. Their presence explained the sirens she thought she'd heard.

"Everyone okay?" Mike Simone, dressed in full fire-fighting gear, stepped into the classroom. "You should have told me this is what you had planned for my cup-cakes."

"I'm sorry. This is all my fault." Maddie accepted the blanket Mike handed her. In her mind she envisioned what could have been the finished product. Rows of delicious cupcakes with delicate lace wrappers would have been an impressive last class. Instead, a mushy mess was all Brad would have to write about.

Mike glanced at the burned mitt on the floor and the charred pan in the sink. "Obviously a kitchen fire. We see these all the time. Good thing the center installed a sprinkler system. These fires can get out of control."

Maddie felt terrible. She had been so involved in her personal thoughts, she hadn't thought about what all this would do to the center's already strained budget.

"Nothing we can do now," Brad said. "Some of the kitchen crew at Nona's might be willing to help out with the cleanup. They have some experience with this kind of thing."

"The guy's right," Mike agreed. He extended a gloved hand to Brad. "I'm Mike Simone. I made those cupcakes."

"I know who you are. I wrote a piece about your dual careers." Brad shook Mike's hand. "Brad Angelo, food writer."

Mike looked at Maddie and chuckled. Then he turned to Brad and said, "That was a nice piece you wrote about my shop."

"Okay, male bonding over." She stepped between the two men. "Don't you have some fireman stuff you need to do?"

"Sure do," Mike said, then added, "Let's get the two of you out of here so we can make sure none of the ashes are still smoldering."

Before being ushered out the door, Maddie rushed over to the desk and retrieved her shopping bags. Anxious that the water had damaged her purchases, she peeked in the bags and released a sigh of relief. Everything appeared untouched by the sprinkler shower.

"Something important?" Brad put his arm around her waist and attempted to look inside.

"My dress for tomorrow."

"I can hardly wait." He smiled. "I'm anticipating another eventful night."

Maddie couldn't return his smile. Her stomach did a flip. A flip that had nothing to do with his enticing smile and everything to do with what could happen at the party.

Chapter Ten

When Maddie opened her door to greet Brad it was obvious the huge box in his arms did not contain chocolates or a corsage.

"I've had this lying around for a while and thought you might like it." He watched Maddie tear the brown wrapping off the box.

"An espresso machine?" This was better than chocolate or flowers. She hadn't had a decent cup of espresso since she left Zest.

"I get my fill at Nona's." Brad shrugged. "Anyway, the girls keep me too busy to indulge in such luxuries at home."

"I don't know what to say. No one has ever given me such a great gift." Maddie put the machine on the kitchen counter. "Thank you." She walked over to Brad and gave him a light peck on his cheek. She was all too aware of the tight space in her kitchen and couldn't move until he did.

Brad took her hand and gently pulled her closer. His

great-aunt's soap, his thoughtful gift, and her hand in his made her senses spin.

She glanced up at him. Were they going to be delayed in getting to the party?

Over her shoulder Brad looked at the wall clock. "Hey, we better go if we want to make our grand entrance." With her hand still in his he led her out of the kitchen toward the front door.

Grand entrance, Maddie thought. The words buzzed in her ear. She was hoping to be as inconspicuous as possible at this party.

Neil Enzo greeted all his guests with a gusto that made each one feel like a celebrity. He knew everyone in the industry, all the gossip, and never forgot a dessert or a favorite chef. Maddie, who fell into the latter category, had been avoiding him since her arrival.

Very few people knew that Neil had gone from financier to chocolatier, or that he had been an assistant sous chef to Maddie Higgins. They had both started at the bottom of the food chain. Their talent and ingenuity helped them move up. In spite of their humble starts, Neil was now at the top and Maddie felt as insignificant as a crumb on the floor.

She and Brad made their way to the buffet table. Polite chatter hummed around them. People smiled at her and she smiled back. Some of them looked twice and whispered behind their napkins. She ignored them, concentrating instead on the elegant displays. The best part

was that they were all made with some kind of chocolate. Maddie took a deep breath. The sights and smells
helped rid her of any uneasy feelings.

She watched Brad circle the table studying one decadent food choice after another. Tiered trays offered
mini pan quiches with chocolate and nuts. Chefs carved
chocolate glazed roast beefs. Best of all were the steam-
ing bowls of meatballs simmering in a cocoa-based
sauce.

"Taste this." Maddie took a bite and offered the rest
to Brad. "They remind me of the meatballs on the cover
of your cookbook."

"The book you so reluctantly purchased the night we
met." Brad leaned in past the meatball and put his arm
around her waist. Pulling her close, he gently kissed her
lips. "Pure ecstasy. A perfect blend of sweet and spicy."

His thigh rested against hers, pressing the cool silky
lining of her dress against her skin. A gentle shiver ran
through her. Overstimulated by familiar scents, Brad's
closeness, and his soft kiss, Maddie hadn't been this happy
in a long time. This might be the time to tell the truth.
She opened her mouth to speak. Brad held up a hand to
silence her.

"I know you were trying to get away from me that
evening and I have no idea why," he whispered against
her lips. "I'm just glad you showed up again."

"You're the one who kept reappearing." Maddie took
a step back.

"Is that bad?" A playful smile curled his lips. "I haven't

felt this way about anyone since my divorce. We work well together. Don't you agree?"

"Yes," she whispered, unsure how he was going to react when he discovered why she had been running away from him that night. So much had changed since their first meeting.

"Listen." He rubbed her bare shoulder, sending sparks down the length of her arm. "I'll admit I'm still curious, but I'm not going to ask. I'm sure you have a good reason for not sharing your thoughts that evening."

Feeling too good to let the past affect this moment, she forced a smile and turned her attention to the food. It was at that moment she spotted Neil walking toward them.

"Oh my god." His timing couldn't have been worse. She couldn't hide the entire evening.

"Maddie Higgins. Where have you been?" Neil threw his arms around her, sending a surprised Brad back a few steps. "The buzz in the industry was that you had left New York."

"Obviously not true." She offered a tilted smile.

"I tried to call you as soon as I heard about that unfortunate experience."

"I wasn't taking calls." Her phone had rung off the hook for days after Brad's review. She knew there was no way to weed out the gloaters from the people who were genuinely concerned. Not answering calls turned out to be the best option.

"That's all in the past. And look at you." Neil spun her

around. "You're looking even more beautiful than before. And the sparkle in your eyes is amazing."

Maddie followed Neil's glance in Brad's direction. With his arms crossed, he leaned casually against the table. His expression was one of amusement mixed with an edge of shock. The sly turn at the corner of his mouth enhanced his dimple. The sight of that dimple usually made her heart flutter. Instead, a cold chill ran up her back. This was the moment she had been dreading. The confidence she'd had moments ago churned with the meatball in her stomach. The conversation was about to turn sour.

"Did you come with Brad Angelo?" Neil asked.

At an Enzo party everyone needed an invitation or to be invited as a plus one. Although it would have been easier to suggest she was a party crasher, she owed it to Neil to explain that there had been no breach in his security.

"Yes." She gave a noncommittal shrug. "Brad Angelo invited me tonight."

"The same Brad Angelo who wrote about your unfortunate experience?" Neil raised a brow.

Unable to form the word *yes,* she shook her head up and down.

Brad stepped out of the shadows and placed his arm around Maddie. "Unfortunate event?" he asked.

"Oops." Neil glanced from Brad to Maddie, noticing Brad's possessive grip. "You two appear amicable. I assume you smoothed out the chocolate lumps in your sudsy relationship." Neil laughed and excused himself as he rushed off to welcome a glamorous couple in matching black tuxedos. Maddie was left with an astonished Brad.

"You know Neil Enzo?" Brad's dark eyes hazed over with disbelief. "What is he talking about? Unfortunate experience, chocolate lumps, sudsy relationship? Has the man lost his mind?"

Maddie bit her lip. "I was afraid this would happen when I accepted your invitation," she replied in a barely audible whisper. The moment of reckoning had arrived. Her knees felt weak and her heart was about to beat out of her chest.

"Neil and I go way back." Maddie thought that would be a good place to start her story.

"You know Neil Enzo?" Brad asked again. He looked at her as if he were seeing her for the first time. "Do we need to talk?"

"It might take a while." Maddie searched for a sign of help in the crowded room. Obviously the cavalry was not going to arrive. She let Brad usher her toward a table away from the other guests.

A passing waiter offered them chocolate martinis. Masking her inner turmoil, Maddie reached for two glasses. She placed them on the table.

She didn't wait for Brad to pull out her chair. She sank into her seat and tried to review the whole set of events that had led up to this evening. After months of self-imposed hibernation, she stepped out of her apartment and crossed paths with the man who had overwhelmed her with feelings of revenge. And now she sat across from him, unsure how she was going to explain she no longer hated him.

Brad waited silently. He reached for one of the martini glasses. Maddie tensed. She watched his lips touch the rim. Her thoughts became clouded with that horrid image. The rim had been dipped in chocolate sauce and, of all things—powdered sugar.

The ugly memories she had suppressed began to surface. Right here, in front of the chocolate culinary world, she was about to watch Brad choke. Would it be her fault again?

"Don't drink that!" she shouted a little too loud, attracting the attention of a passing waiter.

"Is something wrong?" The waiter's voice brought her back to the present.

"No." She dismissed the waiter with a wave of her hand and turned her attention back to Brad.

When she looked across the table she almost laughed out loud. Relieved that she didn't see a red choking face, she fought to regain her composure. In reality, a handsome man with strong fingers wrapped around a delicate martini glass stared back.

"Why not? It looks good." Brad stopped with his glass held in midair.

"It's just that I need your full attention." Ignoring her own advice, Maddie reached for her glass. She took a huge sip. Chocolate was a fixer for everything. The perfect combination of the sweet chocolate and martini blend would be her truth serum.

Brad straddled the chair across from her. He looked perplexed. She imagined this look was probably the same one he gave the girls while waiting for an explanation of some seven-year-old antic.

Maddie felt about as mature as a kid caught with the cookie jar, but she was an adult with an adult problem that only she could resolve.

"Just before Neil joined us we were discussing the night we met at your book signing." Having no carefully planned explanation, she waited for some form of acknowledgment.

Brad only nodded.

"You know, I didn't plan to get in the line for your autograph." She bit her lip and fiddled with the rim of her glass.

"We've established that." Brad had grown serious. "I guess I should be interested in what you were thinking or who the real Maddie Higgins is."

"It's not about me, now. It's about who I used to be."

"Who were you?"

"You sound like a reporter."

"I am."

"What I mean is—it's more complicated than who or what I am." Maddie released an exasperated sigh. "It was all about the review you wrote about my signature dessert."

"You have a signature dessert?"

Maddie nodded and continued. "About six months ago you ate at Zest."

"Are you kidding? The twins keep my head in such a spin, I don't remember what I had for breakfast this morning. You expect me to remember what I ate six months ago."

"Oh, I'm sure you remember a certain dessert you reviewed."

"I don't do reviews on a regular basis." Brad rubbed his hand through his hair.

"Luckily for the pastry chefs of New York." Maddie forced a laugh. "But you do remember the review you wrote that night?" She glanced at him from the corner of her eye, hoping for a divine intervention that would somehow exonerate her. "It was a review of a torta di chocolate."

"There's one dessert I'll never forget. It almost killed me." Brad smacked an open palm on the table. "You made the soap powder torta. *You're* the pastry chef responsible for my trip to the ER?"

"This is going to be more difficult than I imagined." Maddie steadied the jiggling martini glasses. "It was supposed to be a light dusting of powdered sugar."

After all these months it should have felt good to finally say out loud what she had only been able to recreate in her vivid imagination, but it didn't. Geraldine had said that when it happened, it would be her epiphany. The words should have been therapeutic, leaving Maddie with a feeling of euphoria. Instead she felt a terrible new sense of doom.

Brad looked at the sugar-coated rim of the martini glass. His glare was anything but sweet. "You waited all this time to tell me?" He pushed the glass to the center of the table.

"It got complicated."

"I was rushed to the ER, given multiple shots, and almost ended up with a tube down my throat. *That* was complicated." His expression darkened with an unreadable message.

Maddie cringed. "We sent a busboy to the hospital as soon as we realized what had happened."

"A busboy."

"Someone had to explain the situation." Maddie twisted her hands together.

"Maybe someone of a little more importance should have followed to apologize."

"Are you suggesting *I* should have come to the hospital?" In her haste to tell the truth, had she revealed too much?

"You might have avoided the soap powder review if you had."

"I was in the kitchen investigating, trying to figure out what had happened."

Brad looked away. Momentarily speechless, he watched the other guests.

"I know this is a lot for you to digest at one time." She wished he would say something, anything, to break the uncomfortable silence that compelled her to chatter on like a senseless idiot. "I didn't actually add the soap powder," she said, even though redirecting the blame had never made her feel better about the incident. "But it was my dessert. I was the pastry chef. I should never have allowed that torta to leave the kitchen."

"That's reassuring," Brad snapped. He shifted in his chair. The movement made her tense. Would he suggest she leave? He had every right to.

"I would have explained, but your review was in the morning paper. I had already lost my job." She took a deep breath and tried to relax. His reaction should not have surprised her. She had hoped he would have become a bit more forgiving with the passing of time.

"Maybe you should have tried to contact me." He threw the torta back at her.

Maddie tried to imagine how all this must look to him. Honesty was his motto. She had deceived him. From his point of view she must appear untrustworthy. He had accurately reported the incident and she was the one who had suffered the long-term consequences.

Brad stood up. Maddie feared he would walk away feeling let down. She didn't want this to be the end of their relationship. Reaching out, she placed a hand on his upper arm. His muscle twitched under her fingers, but he didn't pull away.

"Would you have been willing to listen?" Maddie asked.

He turned. Something flickered in his eyes. "If I had

seen you face-to-face it would have been difficult to associate you with such a horrid experience." He cupped her chin, turning her face upward. "Why didn't you reveal who you were when we met?"

His touch cascaded through her. She felt that now-familiar sensation of melting to the spot. "I thought I'd never see you again. And if I did, I planned to get revenge for the way your review had turned my life upside down." Her confessions rolled off her tongue like chocolate drops.

"But you did see me." Brad hesitated. "Your life doesn't seem so bad at the moment, but you almost ended mine. I can't believe it took you so long to tell me we had a connection."

"Aren't you being a bit dramatic?" Maddie didn't want to sound so defensive, but Brad was not being very kind. "You recovered the next day. I lost six months of my life and my career."

"You want me to pretend like it never happened? It's too late to print a retraction."

"You could try and be a little more understanding. I'm willing to forgive the horrid words you wrote about me because meeting you has turned my life around. You've helped me get back on track and even find my lost muse."

"This is more serious than some lost muse." Brad's eyes blazed like a pan ignited with brandy. "I went into this relationship thinking you were someone else."

Although Maddie sensed that he felt deceived, she

had expected kinder words. Couldn't he see that where they were now was more important than what had happened or who she had been back then?

"What happened to what you said earlier?" She offered a reminder. "You were curious, but it no longer mattered."

"I said that before I knew all the facts."

"Facts," Maddie retorted. "Is it always about the facts?"

"Facts never lie."

"Maybe I should leave. After all, you're the one with the invitation and a story to write." She didn't want to leave, but if someone had to go it should be her. She didn't want to step back into the world without Brad. "Why should the evening turn out to be a failure for both of us."

"The evening is far from a failure." His tense jaw betrayed a sense of shock. "I've discovered the real Maddie Higgins—not that I'm completely surprised. I always suspected you had some chocolate talent." His tone sounded tired and low, compelling her to stay where she stood.

"What's done is done." Maddie had thought she would never be able to forgive him. But the unwelcome tension between them made it obvious *she* was now the one seeking forgiveness for misleading him.

"You appear to have some very influential friends." Brad nodded in Neil's direction. "You could have gotten another job."

"No one in the industry would touch me." Maddie released an exasperated sigh. "I've been unemployed except for a few odd jobs here and there. The teaching job at the community center was one of them."

"Who did you pretend to be when the director hired you?"

"I told the truth. She didn't seem to care."

"I told the truth too," Brad said. "Your dessert was deadly."

"Now that I know you, I understand that's what you do best. You report things honestly." She never questioned his integrity, just his choice of words. "Did you have to refer to my best dessert as the 'soap powder torta'?"

"I thought it was pretty clever considering what I had gone through. It was a wonder I could think at all."

"I can't believe you're defending the review." Maddie wanted to shout at him. "You have no idea how much I disliked you."

"So you hated me?" He baited her. "You wanted revenge?"

"For months, but I'm not a hateful person. I saw a therapist. Well, not exactly a therapist. Geraldine's my happiness life coach."

"Did she help you find happiness?"

She could hear a hint of amusement in his voice.

"Geraldine helped me understand what I was going through." To herself she acknowledged, *You helped me find happiness.*

"Are you still out for revenge?" He stepped closer and touched her arm, then quickly crossed his arms over his chest.

"You're a hard guy to dislike." She fought her over-whelming need to confess her true feelings. This wasn't the time to admit she had fallen in love with the man she had vowed to revenge. At this moment she doubted he would care.

Chapter Eleven

Brad sank into a chair. When had he become the bad guy in this scenario? He had written some articles in the past that might have rubbed a few people the wrong way, but no one had sought revenge. If Maddie's idea of revenge was linked to his growing attraction to her, she had succeeded. She had unlocked his closely guarded heart. Had she planned it this way?

He watched models covered in chocolate ribbons move about the party. Sideways, the women were about as thick as a vertical chocolate bar and yet they balanced their headpieces as if they were weightless, creating volume without heft. Their whimsical attire provided a short-lived moment of relief.

Grateful for the distraction, Brad studied them. He wasn't the only man in the room watching the women dressed in seductive cocoa-colored chiffon.

He was far from an expert in the relationship department, but one thing he had learned was that trust was an important component. Maybe he was just as much at fault.

He had suspected Maddie was hiding something: a secret recipe, an infamous past or an ex-boyfriend. If he had followed his reporter's instinct and checked out the facts, Brad might have discovered *he* was the secret. Her inscrutable nature had been an alluring part of her charm. He had no one to blame but himself. He hadn't wanted to replace the mysterious attraction with cold, hard facts.

"They're stunning, aren't they?" Maddie stood off to the side.

Brad's attention shifted back to Maddie. Dressed in her shimmering black dress, she was just as glamorous.

She stared back at him, her chin lifted in a defiant tilt. She wasn't going to let him walk away. Something had been brewing between them and he felt a wave of desire wash over him. He didn't want to lose her, even now that he knew she had been deceiving him.

Brad was good with words; it was what he did for a living. This time it wasn't incumbent on him to find the right words. Maddie was the one who needed to explain, but what else did he want her to say? She had been honest about everything, leaving no chocolate crumb unturned. He appeared to be the one who was at fault for destroying her career.

He watched a photographer stop to take her photo and felt a twinge of jealousy as the man approached.

"Maddie Higgins. Where have you been hiding?" he heard the man greet her. Was Brad the only one who had been in the dark all these weeks?

Maddie glanced at the camera and offered a smile of

recognition. Brad too, recognized the man—Simon Lester, his former colleague and the person responsible for the unsolicited photos of his daughters.

"What have we got here? My old friend, Brad Angelo?" A thin-lipped smile stretched across Simon's lips. Maddie was no longer his prime interest.

Brad made a vain attempt to usher Maddie away, but she tenaciously refused to follow his lead. Okay, maybe he deserved that. What right did he have to dictate who she spoke to even if his reason for diverting her was for her own protection? Maybe she was familiar with Simon's work, but he doubted she knew what a parasite the man had become.

She turned to greet Simon. "Hello, Simon."

"My favorite torta di chocolate." Simon placed a soft kiss on Maddie's cheek, then he turned to Brad and added, "And the man responsible for its demise."

Brad's fist clenched at his side. "You know Maddie?"

"We go way back." Simon plucked a chocolate-covered cherry off a passing tray. "How many years ago did you win top prize at the New York Chocolate Fest?"

"Three years ago," Maddie said.

"I photographed her award-winning torta."

"The torta di chocolate that I ate? Was it covered with soap powder?" Brad wasn't about to let Simon make him the bad guy. Maddie was doing a good enough job on her own of making him feel black-hearted.

"It was a careless oversight on my part." Maddie sighed. "I didn't inspect the dessert before it left the kitchen." She threw her arms in the air. "I'd say we're even."

Brad had let the incident go. If he'd never met Maddie, the torta review would have been just another piece he had written, but the events of the evening were bringing it all back.

"It's been months since the incident and you're very much alive, my old friend." Simon patted Brad on the back and continued. "The world, however, is not the same without her wonderful torta. I followed her career and her rise to chocolate fame." He gave Brad a warning glance. "Then one day—*poof!* She was gone from the culinary world." Simon popped the cherry in his mouth.

Maddie stifled a giggle. She seemed to be enjoying Simon's silly rendition of the notorious review, but Brad wasn't. He realized now he should have shown more interest in the soap powder chef. If he had been covering a story he would have pursued every detail. As a stand-in for the magazine's food critic there seemed no need to go beyond the review.

Maddie and Simon were enjoying this chance meeting. Brad would bet she was a bit bent out of shape by his reaction to her confession. Maybe he should have been more understanding. He never defended anything he wrote because, unlike the man standing in front of him, Brad reported the facts.

To add to the unusual mix, a member of Neil's entourage stopped at Maddie's side. He whispered something in her ear that made her giggle.

"Excuse me, gentlemen. Neil wants to introduce me to someone." She turned and walked to the side of the room, leaving Brad and Simon alone.

Brad stepped back, folded his arms, and studied Maddie. He felt like he was seeing her for the first time. She probably didn't even realize how delicious she looked as she sashayed across the floor. He couldn't deny he liked what he saw, but for over six weeks, she'd been playing a game with him, keeping their connection a secret. Her deceit didn't sit right with him—even if he found her irresistible.

After their first meeting at the community center, he realized now, she had been trying to keep her distance from him. She had wanted him to go away and never learn her true identity. Taking away their encounter at Zest, he didn't think she found him repulsive. She just needed time to get over what had happened. He needed time too, to digest everything she had told him.

Having her disappear from his life because of a few badly chosen words would be terrible. His girls liked her, and his grandmother's menu had a fresh new look because of her. But most of all, he liked being around Maddie Higgins, whoever she was.

"You're looking way too serious." Simon approached.

"Am I?" Brad replied.

Simon followed Brad's gaze to Maddie. "The two of you seem to have reconciled your differences."

"What makes you such an expert?" Brad asked.

"This." Simon turned on the viewer of his camera.

"The camera lens never lies." He showed Brad candid shots he had taken of the guests. He paused when he came to the one of Maddie at the buffet table.

Her disheveled curls appeared a little wild and tangled—as if they were tousled by the wind. Brad smiled.

"You always had a knack for capturing people at their best. I'll give you that." Intrigued by the shot, Brad waited to see the next one and the next and the next. There were photos of Maddie from the moment she entered the room. "Wow, you've got lots of pictures of Maddie."

"She always made a good subject." Simon stepped back, a hint of a blush on his pudgy cheeks. "And so did her chocolate."

"These photos have nothing to do with chocolate. They're all about Maddie." Brad hid his surprise, not wanting to complicate this already awkward situation. "Was there ever anything between you?"

"I was never that lucky. She's amazing, in case you haven't noticed. There's an energy about her when she's creating a new dessert that makes it hard not to want her as much as her decadent chocolate." Simon sighed. "What a way to end your meal as well as your evening."

"Hey, watch it. She's still my date." Brad gave Simon a warning glare. Everything about her was beginning to make sense. Her excitement when she worked with chocolate had been contagious. She had thrilled not only his girls with her cannoli competition, giant cookies, and inspiring suggestions, but Brad as well.

"Don't worry, buddy, her desserts are all I've ever

been privileged to," Simon said, then asked, "When did you two get together?"

Brad remained silent, choosing not to explain the situation.

"I get it. You're not talking," Simon said. "I've been following your series about the generational cooking class. Nice articles."

"Are you complimenting my work?" Brad wished this guy would take his camera and crawl back into the lens.

"We used to work well together. Your articles and my photos were a winning combination." Simon didn't have to remind Brad how their work complemented each other. "Why no pictures of the class? Couldn't you find a photographer whose work was up to your high standards?" Simon chuckled.

"The teacher's request." Brad directed his attention across the crowded room. Maddie listened attentively to the man standing next to her.

Simon followed his gaze. "Wait a minute. I get it." A look of understanding lit up Simon's face. "Maddie taught that class. She wouldn't want any photos." He snapped his fingers and pointed at Brad. "You had no idea who she was. You never saw the chef who made the soap powder torta."

Brad cringed. The words "soap powder torta" sounded harsh coming from Simon's mouth.

"When did she tell you who she was?" Simon continued his barrage of questions.

"Why don't you just stick to taking pictures? You were never any good at investigative reporting."

"But you are the expert." Simon clapped his hands together. "Oh man, I love this. The infamous Brad Angelo let his investigative powers slip for a pretty face."

"You're right. I just found out tonight that I wrote the review that destroyed her career."

"And how does it make you feel?"

"Since when did you become a therapist?"

"I'll tell you how you feel. You feel like a louse and it bothers you."

"Of course it bothers me. She could have told me who she was weeks ago."

"Oh, this is better than I thought. Maddie Higgins gets one up on Brad Angelo, a writer who built his reputation on honest, concise reporting. Did you ever think she was afraid that you would react negatively when she revealed her secret?"

Brad's thoughts had been short-sighted, consumed with his feelings of betrayal. Instinctively, he'd reacted to protect himself, never giving a thought to how difficult this had been for Maddie. Was he willing to lose her over this?

Looking across the room, he watched Maddie and Neil talking to the small group that had gathered around them. A man in a sparkling black jacket said something to Maddie. Brad recognized the look of pleasant surprise on her face. Everyone stopped talking. He kept his eyes on her face, wondering what was of such great importance that all eyes had turned toward Maddie.

Neil turned and signaled for Simon and Brad to join them. Simon rushed forward, while Brad hesitated. Whatever was going on, this appeared to be Maddie's circle. He didn't belong there anymore. He took a thick chocolate beverage off a passing tray and took a long sip. The rich liquid held a hint of raspberry liqueur. Brad had avoided anything raspberry since the incident at the Chocolate Boutique. He waited, expecting the worst. When nothing happened, relief coursed through him. He took it as a positive sign and walked off to join the group.

The conversation had an excited energy.

Neil turned to Maddie and asked, "Are you up to being a competitor?"

"I haven't been very creative lately." She turned to Brad and filled him in. "I've just been asked to be a chef on a TV cooking competition."

A pain squeezed his heart. Maddie had been welcomed back into the fold. Everything about her radiated excitement at the prospect of being on a TV cooking show. What would that mean for their relationship?

"So what do you think?" Neil clapped him on the back.

Brad looked at Maddie and their eyes met. She wrinkled her nose and shrugged.

"I'm sure she's the perfect candidate for whatever you're planning." Brad knew anything Neil supported would be successful. Maddie might have wanted revenge, but as disappointed as he was with her recent confession, he didn't wish her bad luck. He wanted good things for her.

"He's the critic. He should know." Neil laughed.

"That's for sure," Maddie said.

"This the guy?" Mr. Sparkle Jacket asked.

"Am I what guy?" Brad asked, a bit abruptly.

Neil quickly answered. "Brad, this is Abe Zukini. He produces some very popular cooking competitions."

Zukini? They have to be kidding. Brad suppressed the urge to laugh out loud and assumed his reporter's face: listening, observing, and assessing.

"Call me Abe." Sparkle Jacket extended his hand. "I'm familiar with your work, Mr. Angelo. I enjoyed your articles on the generational cooking class. Wish I had thought of the concept."

"Thank you. I'm sorry I can't return the compliment. I'm afraid my TV viewing is limited to Spongebob and Dora."

"Kids? I've got three. How old are yours?"

"Seven-year-old twins," Brad answered. He should be the one asking these questions.

"I'm surprised you never mentioned the teacher in any of your articles," Abe said. "Some nice old lady from the neighborhood?"

"Actually . . ." Brad looked at Maddie, unsure how much information she wanted revealed. He didn't want to be blamed for anything else this evening. He already felt like a big jerk.

"I taught the class." Maddie, the lady in the chocolate protection program, stepped forward. She answered without any hesitation.

"This is getting better all the time." Abe placed his hand on his chest and honored Maddie with a mock bow. "I'm overwhelmed by the talent in this room."

"So am I," Brad said sarcastically.

"And you should be. Your date happens to be one of my favorite pastry chefs," Neil said.

"That seems to be the general consensus this evening." Brad glanced sideways at Maddie. In spite of her frown, directed at him, she had an air of confidence he hadn't noticed before. Perhaps all the attention and praise from people who knew her before the bad review was the spark she needed. Brad wouldn't interfere, but he wasn't sure where this was all going. To help clear up his confusion he went into interview mode. "What's the next step in your plan for this TV show?"

"Allow me to explain." Abe positioned himself next to Brad. "Maddie's sudden appearance after so many months generated a lot of buzz at this party. I asked around and discovered there was a bad review—bad, but amusing. This stuff makes for good viewing."

The time had come for Brad to own up to his actions. "Regretfully, I'm responsible for all the buzz. I wrote the review. I never imagined it would have such long-term repercussions."

"I love the story. You called her signature dessert a soap powder torta. You're brilliant."

Brad didn't need to see Maddie's face to know how she reacted to Abe's last remark. "Brilliant" was definitely not the word she would have chosen.

"How does the review connect to your TV show?" Brad shook his head in disbelief. Even though he had written several pieces on this form of entertainment, he wasn't a big fan of reality TV food shows. "Maddie is a talented pastry chef. Why remind anyone about her unfortunate experience?"

"Why not? She'll be the underdog, viewers will love her. And with you on the show too, it will have an edge before it even airs."

"I don't recall anyone asking me to participate," Brad said.

"Hey, did you forget I'm standing here?" Maddie turned slowly toward Abe, an astonished look on her face. "Did you ever think of asking me if I want to be part of this package deal?"

Abe glanced at Maddie. "I didn't think you would have a problem with any of this. It's the perfect opportunity to show him what you can do."

Brad waited, hoping Maddie would turn down the offer. Everyone stood by in silence. Maddie looked to be in deep thought, but Brad could tell by the way she bit her lip that she had already made her decision.

"Just tell me where and when you start shooting," Maddie said. "I've got a newly discovered muse waiting to be creative."

"You do understand I need both of you to get this

thing off the ground?" Abe looked from Maddie to Brad.

"I don't bake," Brad said with an edge of sarcasm.

"We're not asking you to bake. You have an uncanny perception about food and a large readership. You're perfect judge material." Abe placed an arm around Brad. "Think of the increase to your readership."

"Me, judge a TV show?" Brad chuckled and glanced behind him as if this character might have been address-ing someone else. This guy was good. He knew just the spots to hit, but agreeing to be part of a TV food show would be time-consuming. Viewers saw everything through the magic of television. But Brad had interviewed cooking show judges. He knew that the decision making could go on forever. Every two-minute explanation seen by viewers had started out as an hour-long culinary lec-ture. Hours, days, and sometimes even weeks could pass before the show was ready to air.

"I've got a lot in the works at the moment." He had his daughters to think about. Balancing the single father thing had just started to fall into place. Another morsel on his plate could upset everything he had worked so hard to achieve. Unsure if he was prepared to make such a commitment, Brad looked over at Maddie. Did she understand the implications?

"You're willing to do this, knowing they're going to air your dirty laundry?" Brad asked.

"I've got nothing to hide anymore." She kept her fea-tures perfectly composed.

"Maddie's game. Can I count on you to close the deal?" Abe asked.

"What are you offering her?" Brad asked.

"There's a ten-thousand-dollar first prize and the moment of fame that goes with just being a contestant." Abe walked away, giving them some time to discuss his offer.

Brad reached for Maddie's hand and led her away from the crowd. Despite the smile of confidence she forced, her body was tense. "Are you willing to expose yourself to millions of viewers for the prize money?" Brad may not have known the true identity of Maddie Higgins, but the Maddie he did know would not be wooed so easily by prize money or fame.

"It's not only for the money. Although heaven knows I could use it." She sighed. "My muse was gone for so long I thought I'd never find it again. I need to prove to myself that it's really back."

"And this competition is the only way?" He dropped her hand and stepped back.

"Yes," she whispered.

She wasn't asking him if he would be part of the team, only explaining why she had to be. He had been deceived. Her confession was still too fresh in his mind. In time he would get over the deception.

Life in general and his divorce had made him a quick healer, but he needed time to resolve the hurt. There was no way to take back his words. The situation at the time had warranted his honest assessment. Life did not always deal you the hand you wanted, but facts were indisputable.

The time had come for Brad to use his investigative skills and discover the real Maddie Higgins.

Things would have been different if their paths had never crossed, but now life without Maddie was not an option. Staying close to her until he gathered all the facts and came to grips with his personal dilemma would be his choice.

The opportunity to be near her had just been handed to him on a chocolate platter. The deal was too tempting to turn down. But he'd make them sweat a little. He didn't want Abe to realize there was so much more to his relationship with Maddie than just a bad review.

Chapter Twelve

The next day, Maddie needed time to digest her over-night rise in popularity. Aside from the fact that she didn't know what Brad was going to decide, she worried that maybe she had been too quick to agree to do Abe's show. Shows like this challenged your talent. They were out to prove the contestants were more than a one-dish wonder. If a chef made a good torta, could they make a better blueberry pie?

Chloe had agreed to meet Maddie at the Chocolate Boutique and run through the events of last night.

"Imagine winning the Pan au Chocolat ribbon?" Chloe sighed.

"The ribbon is an honor, but the prize money will be a big help." Maddie polished the glass countertop in dreamy circular movements.

"Are you still thinking of taking a trip to Belgium?"

"No." Maddie looked around the shop. "I think I'd like a place of my own, a little pastry café."

"Sounds nice, but I could rent you space if you're

really interested." Chloe balanced her very pregnant body on a stool across the counter from Maddie.

"Thanks, but I want enough room to experiment with all kinds of desserts." Maddie placed a tray of sliced fruit dipped in chocolate on the shiny counter.

"Tell me about your evening. Is the producer's name really Abe Zukini?"

Maddie laughed. "It's just a stage name. Neil said Abe's real name is Abe Zuckerman. His debut TV show displayed unusual recipes for zucchini and the name Zukini stuck."

"If you win, you could use a stage name too." Chloe dipped an orange slice into a bowl of melted chocolate.

Maddie reached for a tray of naked chocolate candies. She needed a task like decorating chocolate to help calm her. "Like what, Maddie di Suds?"

"No, I was thinking more like a combination of Maddie and Brad." Chloe dipped another fruit slice. "Maybe Braddie, Maad, or Mrad."

"Isn't that a bit over-the-top?" Maddie interrupted her chocolate swirling and looked at her friend.

"Just a thought." Chloe shrugged. "I don't watch much TV, but the reality-type cooking shows I've seen are rather out there. Are you ready for that?"

"I don't even know if the deal is on."

"Braddie didn't agree last night?" Chloe asked. They laughed so hard they missed the mark on their dipping and swirling.

"Brad and I didn't exactly end the night on pleasant

terms." Maddie composed herself and stood up. "You can imagine his reaction to finding out I made his soap powder torta."

"Was it that bad?" Chloe asked.

"At first, but I can't blame him." Maddie cleaned the counter and moved a finished tray of chocolate-dipped fruits to a table near the window. The street was quiet. She was about to turn back when she spotted Brad coming down the street. The tray hit the table with a clunk.

"Hey, careful with those chocolates." Chloe turned just as Brad opened the door. She gave Maddie a questioning look and announced, "I'm going to put the rest of the fruit in the fridge and straighten up back there."

Maddie managed a nod. Unsure if Brad had resolved his anger toward her, she made an effort to pull herself together as she moved toward the door. "I didn't expect to see you today."

He looked over her shoulder. "Was that Chloe? She hasn't had that baby yet?"

"Any day now." Maddie heard the door to the prep room shut. Her friend had deserted her.

"You were so gung ho about the show last night." He gave her a curious look. "Have you changed your mind?"

"No," she answered without hesitation. His sudden appearance had helped Maddie come to her decision. "This is the right thing for me to get my career back on track."

Weeks ago, she had been convinced that the only way to find her muse was to make Brad eat his words. Then she met his family and Lily. They made her realize that her retribution would be complete when he discovered her true talent. Slowly she had been doing just that, revealing her talent in small irresistible drops. The outcome did not appear to be in her favor.

"My editor and publisher agree it's a great opportunity for the magazine."

"Oh," Maddie said, not wanting to appear overanxious to hear if he was in agreement with his editor.

"I'm willing to give it a shot. I'd like the chance to see you work under pressure, to see the real Maddie Higgins in her element." He tilted his head to get a better look at her.

"One little indiscretion on my end and you're out for blood?"

"No, just the truth," Brad replied.

"I told you the truth. This hasn't been easy for me either."

"If you're going to do the show, things will get tougher. Reality TV can get vicious." He raised a brow and said, "Just say the word and I'll refuse to do it. Remember, we're a package deal. You can blame it on me."

Her heart hammered in her chest. He was giving her the opportunity to turn down the offer. He would take the fall and she would be off the hook. Then what? They walked away from the show and each other.

She looked up at him. This wasn't about just them. "Did you tell Nona and the girls?" She wanted to hear Nona's reaction.

"I ran it by my grandmother. She agreed to help out

with Sophia and Emily if I agree to do it. I wanted to be sure you were still up for it. This Abe character is going to push the limit on this one. Most reality-type shows go for the nice chef, creepy judge thing."

Maddie looked past him out to the street. She felt warm and secure inside the shop. She almost never wanted to leave. Inside the Chocolate Boutique she never had to subject herself to criticism of her work, but she wanted to be more than just a chocolate salesgirl. She wanted to create irresistible chocolate pastries and sell them in her own shop. The win and the prize money could give her the chance.

"I'm willing to take the chance. Are you?" She searched his face for a sign that he really wanted to do this show.

"I seem to have some experience at being the bad guy." He shrugged. "So why not?"

"Your girls will be thrilled." She smiled. "Their dad will be on TV."

"They're going to love watching *us,* together on TV." He returned her smile, and for a second they shared something more important than the show.

"We'll be on opposite sides." There was a tingling in the pit of her stomach. It had nothing to do with the prospect of the competition. Would Brad feel bad if his family became her cheerleaders, even if her dessert was not the winner in his mind?

"We already are. My grandmother is in your court. Nona's a big fan of the Food Network, but an even bigger fan of yours. She said she knew your time would come and everything would work out." He looked at her intently. "Nona knows something I don't? It wouldn't be the first time I was the only one in the dark when it came to you." The lines between his brows told her he didn't like that.

"Brad, I promise you there are no more secrets." Her lips trembled with a need to smile, but doing so might reveal her fellow conspirators—Nona and Lily. They had kept her secret until she was ready to confess. There was no reason to admit they knew her true identity all along.

"You know the judging will be anonymous?"

"I like that." Maddie breathed an audible sigh of relief.

"And you realize we won't be able to see each other until the show airs?"

He didn't sound like a man who was bowing out of a relationship, just one who was licking his wounds.

Last night, after her confession, their future had looked shadowy. Now she wondered if he had agreed because he knew there was no deal without him or because his editor influenced his decision.

"No fraternizing with the judges?" She offered her hand and hoped he could tell she was not giving up on him. Not seeing him until the show was over might be for the best.

"Absolutely no contact." He stepped closer. His hand closed over hers. "It can take days to tape a show."

"Sometimes weeks," she added, feeling the galvanizing

pull of his closeness. She dug her heels in just inches from him. Did his Italian aunt's soap have some kind of magnetic component that drew her closer against her will?

With perfect timing, Chloe waddled in carrying a tray full of her signature candies. "Hi, Brad."

Brad stepped away from Maddie. "I was just leaving. I agreed to judge. Maddie will fill you in on all the details."

"Not without a candy." Chloe offered Brad something off the tray.

"These look too good to eat."

"They are. They're for display," Maddie lied. She moved the tray out of Brad's reach. Chloe was about to object, but Maddie gave her a warning glance. This was not the time to tempt fate. She imagined the buzz in the industry if Brad ended up in the ER again. She couldn't take the chance. Winning this competition would give her career a jolt that no one could take away. Geraldine had said that when Maddie found her muse she would be grounded again. Chocolate was her ground. Whatever happened, her talent and her chocolate creations would always be hers. Bad reviews, reality TV shows, and jobs would come and go.

She watched Brad walk out the door and knew that she wanted him, the girls, and Nona to be part of her ground. But first, she had to win more than the prize money or the ribbon. She had to win back her reputation.

Chapter Thirteen

Maddie tried to put Brad out of her thoughts and concentrate on what was important—winning the competition. Hard as she tried to regroup her focus, thoughts of Brad intruded into her days and nights.

But now, glancing past the glaring lights of the TV cameras, she found it difficult to concentrate on anything but the challenge ahead.

When Maddie signed on, she had no idea how much went into the preparation for taping a cooking competition. There had been publicity shots and commercial takes as well as long lists of rules. The rules forbade discussing the show or fraternizing with the judges or other contestants between tapings.

Abe made a little speech about the expectations of the viewing audience. They expected drama as a side dish.

She watched Brad take his seat between the two other judges. She could swear he was having as hard a time not looking at her as she was not looking at him. The lady to his right, a popular newspaper food critic, never cracked a smile.

Maddie reminded herself that she was just one of the instruments, a cooking utensil that would bring it all together. Her dessert, whatever it was, would be judged anonymously on taste, texture, and presentation. It was better that way. There would be no favoritism; no one could accuse her of having any influence over Brad.

Her mind turned to the other day when Brad had walked into the Chocolate Boutique. He appeared to have gotten over his anger.

Abe came up behind her and startled her back to the present. "Good luck," he whispered. "They're about to start." He gave her elbow a squeeze and added, "You're going to be a star tonight."

Abe stepped away and a booming theatrical voice started the introductions. "Tonight some of the best pastry chefs will compete for the right to wear the prestigious Pan au Chocolat blue ribbon."

Maddie couldn't help but smile. She had gone from chocolate camouflage to full disclosure and the reward was worth it. To wear the Pan au Chocolat ribbon would once again open doors that had been slammed shut. To be called one of the best pastry chefs would be an honor. She was about to find out if she could live up to the praise. The competition would be stiffer than her best-whipped meringue.

Maddie, dressed in her brand-new chef's jacket, felt bland and unbaked next to the other chefs. Tasha, Queen

called Brad's
before the pot

ging her back to

There was no rule
each other. "What

re on the seat." Tasha
ine. "It's like an omen
es, I get lots of inspira-
She handed Maddie the

mumbled, and stared out

ration came from the crowds
through the magazine.
ha took the magazine from her.
model?" Maddie had no idea.
uture was never her thing.
to Brad Angelo."
studied the photo. The twins, she
their dad, but had inherited their
om their stunning mother. They spoke
more like she was some kind of rock
r mother.
inspiration?" Tasha flipped the page.
o." Maddie thought about Sophia's and
rite desserts. They may know how to stuff a

eweled skull cap and brig
name. Style was not Mad-
ite pants and jacket would
e counter.
introductions. Any tidbits
other chefs might give her

een of Bling Bakeshop, is
nd texture," the announcer
's an independent thinker
Her award-winning cakes
Will she be able to work
s rules?"
, had earned his reputation
e spoon. He wore his logo,
olate, on his pocket.
ed in many competitions,
to win the coveted blue

e loop so long she had no
ined to win.
ce the voice announced,
ning torta di chocolate got
ne of our judges."
of the TV crew responded
soft snickers. No big deal.
ledge. There was nothing
ad knew her secret. She
seemed to be handling it

ell. However, something still n?
left her feeling a bit uneasy. S?
plause was for her torta?
realized the camera?
uneasy—surpr?

"Tonigh?
lar fo?
se?

Ye?
her the?
culinary?

A copy o?
A Soap Powa?
features were t?
the cameras.

Brad had tried to?
kind of drama, but Ma?
gether. She had to conc?
forced a smile. Okay, she c?

"Tonight these three chefs?
chocolate, while keeping in m?
diner." The voice continued, "Ou?
is available to them, but to help the?
will all accompany them on a quick sh?
local Creative Foods store. Let's get roll?
is waiting outside. You have thirty minutes?
be back in the limo."

Maddie felt the constraint of the time lim?
what she would prepare, she decided to use? m?
e muc?

---

forget a single detail of the evening. She re?
arms around her and the smoldering thrill?
of chocolate went up in smoke.
the present.

"You got an idea?" Tasha asked, brin?

"A place to start," Maddie replied.
that said the contestants couldn't talk?
about you?"

"I found this magazine lying he?
produced a glossy fashion magaz?
for me. When I decorate my ca?
tion from the latest fashions."
magazine. "Here, take a look?

"Women and clothes," Sa?
the window.

Maddie hoped his inspi?
on the street. She thumbe?

"Hey, stop there." Tas?

"Do you recognize thi?
Unlike Tasha, haute c?

"She was married?

"Really?" Maddie?
decided, resemble?
long, lanky legs fr?
often of her, but?
star and not the?

"Find some?

"I think s?
Emily's favo?

mean cannoli, but the taste was far too sophisticated for their seven-year-old palates. If she wanted her cupcake to appeal to a wide range of dessert eaters, she would need to keep it sweet and simple. A natural fruit sweetener could make all the difference in her entry. Thanks to Tasha and her omen, Maddie now had a direction.

Camera crews filmed them entering the store and would continue throughout the shopping spree. The judges had been invited and would later comment on the chefs' shopping techniques.

Sam, not the type to let anyone get in his way, proved his determination as soon as he rolled out his shopping cart. Ignoring the other shoppers, he rushed past a mother with a baby in her cart. The tips of their carts made contact, rattled, and tilted to the side.

"Ooh!" Maddie cringed. She rushed forward and reached the unsteady shopping cart at exactly the same moment as Brad. He gave her a surprised look. Did he doubt her compassion? Did he think she would rush by, more worried about the time limit than the possibility that the baby could be injured?

Losing precious seconds, she watched him hand the baby to a grateful mother.

He turned to Maddie and whispered, "You better get going."

Behind him, the young mother asked, "Is there anything I can do for you? I know this store like the back of my hand."

An idea came to Maddie. There wasn't anything in the

rules that said she couldn't ask for assistance. It could take her hours to search the aisles for her ingredients. This young mother would know exactly where to find a healthy choice that would make Maddie's cupcakes just what the judges ordered.

Over her shoulder Maddie spotted the judges watching her. They all looked rather serious, unsure if she was breaking any rules. Only Brad, steadying the shopping cart, seemed amused by her interaction with her new ally.

"What are you looking for?"

"A natural baby product." Maddie made sure no one was in hearing distance.

"Follow me." The grateful young woman handled the aisles like a pro. "Any particular kind of food?"

"A fruit." Maddie and the camera crew followed the shopping cart. "Baby peaches, pears, or a combination will work with what I have planned."

Flour, sugar, chocolate. Maddie made a mental list of the other ingredients she would need. All those ingredients would be waiting back at the studio kitchen. The store was large and time-consuming to navigate. As she passed the produce aisle she grabbed some apples and pears. The chocolate-covered fruit in the display case at the Chocolate Boutique came to mind. She'd think of a way to incorporate the fruit into her dessert on the ride back.

The shopping was complete and all three chefs stood in line to pay for their purchases.

That was the first time she noticed Simon with his

spell.
mme-
mouse
one of
e one of
ggle and
assistant
caped un-

a commo-
lenched the
ould clobber
and waited as

wrong turn and
ached for a fry-
white dishes.
again, the mouse

rew announced. "I
studio one. They're
him this time." Abe
a disapproving look.
s gone."

Ca
meant w
ks ago, the old
ring such non-
ined Maddie
r. There was

a crew and
wary look.
; but they
nowledg-
ate.
f how
t be held
o when
air her
ppy
cup-
ack
on
o

...ve she...

...the next cou...

...e in Tasha's direction...

...spotted the cause of the ruck...

...n a chef hat running across the unb...

Tasha's ramekins? His tiny footprin...

her eccentric designs. Maddie supp...

wondered if Tasha saw the patter...

tossed a towel over the little creatur...

harmed.

How could one little creature cr...

tion? Where had it come from? M...

long handle of her spoon. Unsure i...

the intruder or let it run off, she wa...

the critter made a floury escape.

The unsuspecting little chef mad...

Sam did not hesitate like Maddie. H...

ing pan and smashed it over one of...

"My crust!" Tasha screamed. On...

escaped, but her ramekin shattered...

"I've got him," one of the camera...

thought I put this little guy back in...

filming a commercial. He's the sta...

"Well, make sure you get rid of...

intervened and gave the cameram...

"No problem, sir. He's as good...

The clocks were still ticking. Tasha stared at the on her counter: flour, shattered dishes, and tiny foo prints.

Maddie needed to get back to work. They couldn't stand around and watch precious baking time slip away. Anyone who had worked in a busy kitchen knew that teamwork was what kept it going. If Tasha threw in the towel, a two-chef competition would not be as interesting. Maddie had too much at stake to let that happen.

She and Lily reached for towels, and to her surprise, Sam and his sous chef pitched in too. Fortunately Tasha had layered several other ramekins with her almond crust. They were securely positioned on the back counter, away from all the commotion. She wouldn't have much catching up to do.

Too bad Brad wasn't there to witness the little setback. This was just the kind of material he used in his articles. He would find a clever way to write about the little intruder without alarming his readers. There she was, thinking about him again.

Brad had written about her last class and never mentioned the fire. He had written about kitchen safety instead. The same held true for his unfortunate experience at the Chocolate Boutique. He had written about his own lack of diligence and how stuffing too many candies with strange fillings down his throat had sent him to the ER.

Maddie tossed the remains of the broken dish into the trash and returned to her counter. To help clear her

...nts she went back to work. She stirred the batter one ...st time and poured it into the cupcake tray. Precious minutes had been lost. She might have to forgo a decorative wrapper. Her topping would have to be so outstanding that no one would notice she left the sides of her cupcakes undressed.

The sliced apples and pears were ready for the oven. Once the timer was set Maddie turned her attention to Lily and the chocolate melting in the double boiler. The chocolate would cover just the tips of the baked pears and apples.

The studio kitchen filled with a mixture of wonderful aromas. The camera crew inhaled and smiled. Even Abe seemed affected by the delightful smells.

Time ticked away. The cupcakes were baked, cooled, and ready for their cream cheese frosting. Grateful for the help, Maddie left the frosting for Lily while she removed the fruit from the oven.

Only twenty minutes to go. The fruit had to cool before the ends were dipped in chocolate. Maddie had a vision of each cupcake being topped with a dipped apple and pear slice. A bite into the cake would release the flavor of the jarred baby fruits she had mixed into the batter. Healthy and delicious, her vision of the dessert was definitely a contender for the blue ribbon. She removed the fruit from the oven and waited for the delicate slices to cool.

Time constraints were never good when baking. Anything could happen, as Tasha's unexpected visitor proved.

Tasha stood at the oven tapping her foot, as if that make her crusts bake faster. Maddie wondered what s. planned to fill the ramekins with.

At the far end of the stage, Sam removed his molds from the oven and turned them onto a plate. While they cooled he prepared a pastry bag. Everyone appeared to be at the same hurry-up-and-wait stage.

With a fingertip, Maddie tested the temperature of an apple slice. It felt cool. She carefully lifted it off the parchment and dipped an end in the chocolate. The baked apple slid from her grasp. She stared in disbelief as the apple slice disappeared into the bowl. She was sure the camera had caught that.

"Put the fruit in the freezer for a few seconds," Lily said, in response to Maddie's sigh of exasperation. "It'll be easier to work with."

"Good idea." Maddie acknowledged her with a smile. In a few seconds the fruit was more manageable, but the chocolate was too drippy, creating big "feet" at the end of the fruit slices. Feet on dipped anything were a sign of an amateur. She hadn't subjected herself to ridicule about her torta to let anyone think she was inept.

Ignoring the huge kitchen clock that stared down at her, she moved ahead at a swift pace. She'd plate the frosted cupcakes while the chocolate set on her fruit. With minutes to go, she and Lily reached for paring knifes and cut around the drippy feet. After topping each cupcake with a footless chocolate-dipped apple and pear, they stood back and took deep breaths.

...testants, your time is up," the unseen but ever-...sent voice announced.

Maddie threw her hands in the air. A release of tension cascaded through her. For the moment, everything was done.

Simon, his camera intact, rushed forward and photographed the completed desserts before they were carried off to the judges. "That looks good enough to eat," he said, and winked at Maddie.

When she'd worked at Zest, Simon had been one of her biggest fans. It wasn't that his opinion didn't matter, but his compliment did little to calm her nerves.

Nestled between Sam's flourless chocolate berry cake and Tasha's sparkling amaretto fruit tart sat Maddie's cupcake crowned with chocolate-dipped fruit. The chefs complimented each other on their accomplishments and were dismissed for the evening. They had worked hard, but they all knew the real challenge waited behind closed doors.

Chapter Fourteen

Today was the final taping. Maddie had no time to ease into her day with a cup of espresso and the morning paper. Tired, but inspired by what the day could bring, she arrived at the studio before the other contestants.

Last evening, her phone had never stopped ringing. Nona, Chloe, and Geraldine—everyone wanted to know about the competition. Even if her contract had allowed her to speak about the show, Maddie wouldn't speculate about the results. They would have to wait and watch. The winner would be announced on live TV. Abe wanted to capture surprise as well as disappointment.

Maddie wore her whites again. Only today she wore a sparkly pink cap, compliments of Tasha. When Sam arrived, he also wore a Tasha cap in blue. Tasha had sent them each a cap via a special courier as her way of thanking them for their part in saving her tarts. Abe liked the touch. He took it as a sign of solidarity as the chefs prepared to face the judges. There were rumors flying around

163

studio that it had taken until two AM for the judges to agree on the winner.

Through the magic of television the three desserts appeared on the screen, uneaten. Clips of their preparation were played for the viewing audience.

The judges filed into the studio. Maddie tried to control the dizzy feeling racing through her. Brad crossed the stage with purpose and took his seat. Judging into the early hours of the morning had taken its toll, leaving dark circles under his eyes.

She hadn't seen him or had any contact with him in over a week. Could that be the reason for her hammering heart? He had shaved, and as he passed she caught a familiar whiff of his aunt's wonderful soap.

Maddie and the competition faced the judges, anxious to hear the verdict. She forced herself not to constantly look in Brad's direction. Every nerve quivered with anticipation. Of course she wanted to win, but even more she wanted Brad to acknowledge her talent.

The judges critiqued Sam's flourless chocolate berry cake first.

There was praise for his presentation, some disagreement over the appeal of the texture of a flourless cake, but two to one the judges liked the taste. Everyone agreed he had produced a dessert within the guidelines of the competition.

Brad was the first judge to critique Maddie's cupcake. He smiled and his tired eyes twinkled with approval, or was that just wishful thinking?

"At first I thought Chef Higgins had ple a dessert for her talent." She was sure the Italian accent was charming the TV viewers.

She waited to hear what else he had to say. Tension tightened every muscle in her body.

A smile played on his lips. "After the first taste, I realized the delicate balance between the baby fruit and the cake were perfect." He looked to the other judges, who nodded in agreement. "This is just the kind of dessert that appeals to today's health-conscious diner."

Maddie looked away. Her cheeks felt warm. She hoped no one else noticed.

Brad hadn't finished. "However, I almost considered the chocolate-dipped fruit on top of the frosting a dessert on its own. It was almost overkill."

Seeing him alive and well after eating her dessert should have been reward enough, but Maddie felt the pinch of his criticism. Biting back a defense, she forced a smile and nodded.

The announcer read her thoughts. "Chef Higgins' dessert appears to have had a somewhat positive impact on our first judge. Hopefully he will forgive her past oversights and move on with a favorable review."

The night of Neil's party she had thought that Brad would never forgive her for keeping her secret. If everyone knew that Brad's feelings had nothing to do with what had happened at Zest so many months ago, would the announcer's comments have as much impact?

The next judge, a serious-looking critic, waited for

announcer to finish speaking. "I disagree. I think the chocolate-dipped fruit, if tasted first, is a preview for the delicate fruity taste of the cupcake."

Judge number three, a cookbook author, had something entirely different to say. "If I were making this cupcake I would have gone with a lighter topping. Perhaps a glaze instead of the whipped cream cheese frosting."

Judge two came back with sort of a compliment. "I tend to agree about the frosting. I'm sick of overdone gooey desserts, but this frosting was light enough for my tastes."

At this point, Maddie heard only scattered words and phrases. The lights, the voices, and Brad's fixed smile were becoming a blur. She needed to focus, get herself back to the moment. The judges were being fair, offering constructive criticism, but she couldn't tell if they liked her dessert better than the others.

Tasha, the last contestant to be critiqued, shifted from side to side. Maddie felt her anxiety and wished she could offer a comforting word.

The cookbook author went first. "For presentation, Chef Tasha's Amaretto fruit tart is by far the best. I would love it for the cover of one of my cookbooks. The berries and the light dusting of colored sugar make it sparkle like a Christmas window at Macy's. I was afraid to disturb the beautiful presentation. But I did eat it."

"I agree," the serious judge said. "Once I tasted the tart I felt the need to finish every last morsel, because the chef worked so hard on the stunning presentation."

Maddie had to agree; Tasha's multicolored tart beautiful. How did anyone ever cut into her cakes?

Brad liked the bling. "This is a health-conscious dessert I might be able to convince my girls to taste. However, the custard under the berries was disappointing. I expected excellent, but got only good."

To increase the suspense for the viewers, the contestants were ushered out. The judges would continue bickering back and forth before announcing the winner.

The uncertainty was maddening.

Sam paced back and forth. "I've done lots of these TV competitions. You can usually tell who the judges decided on way before the end of their rambling, but this time . . ." He shrugged. "I haven't got a clue. Does anyone?"

Maddie and Tasha shook their heads. No one exuded confidence over the other contestants. Maddie didn't envy the judges. She would bet all the desserts tasted as good as they looked.

Fifteen minutes backstage seemed like fifteen hours. The judges were not looking for something new. They wanted something just right for today's healthy eater. Maddie was sure she had gotten it right, but so had the other contestants.

With solemn expressions, the three chefs walked back onto the set.

Sam was the first to be excused. Past memories of waiting for the announcement that her torta di chocolate had won the New York Chocolate Fest filled her mind.

night she had stood with Chloe and waited. Tonight Lily was offstage and Brad sat only a few feet away, but she had never felt more alone. So much was riding on this win.

The cookbook author had been chosen to speak for the judges. "Ladies, the decision to pick the winner was not easy." She clasped her hands together and glanced at the other judges. Her perplexed look added drama to the moment. "I would happily order any of the three desserts presented tonight."

Yeah, right, okay, we get it. Maddie was about to jump out of her skin. She wanted to shout at the procrastinating woman with the blue ribbon in her hand.

Finally the judge announced, "Chef Tasha wins the blue ribbon."

Disappointed, Maddie watched Tasha accept the ribbon. The competition had been tough and any one of the chefs deserved to win.

What was it? Was Brad right? Was Maddie's dessert too simple, or was it the cream cheese frosting? Did the chocolate-dipped fruit really distract from the main cake? Maddie's disappointment vanished as she found relief in no longer being the center of attention. She had every reason to be proud of her accomplishment. Geraldine would be proud that she had not held on to her negative feelings.

Maddie was ushered to the wings, where Lily embraced her as if she had won. "A runner-up to Tasha, Queen of Bling, is as good as a win."

Sam congratulated her and echoed Lily's w

"You're as much a star as the winner."

Maddie soon discovered the truth in Sam's words. Abe approached. He handed Maddie an envelope. "Go ahead, open it," he urged. "You didn't know there was a prize for the runner-up as well?"

Inside Maddie found a check for five thousand dollars. Speechless, she shook her head. There might not be a ribbon to hang in her new shop, but this would give her a nice head start.

The cameras stopped rolling. Tasha rushed toward her, suffocating her with a giant hug. Then she threw her arms around a reluctant Sam. "I could have never won without your unselfish help."

Maddie stepped back and watched Tasha enjoy her glory. She could never imagine herself handling it so graciously.

She spotted Brad leaning against the wall with arms crossed over his chest and walked toward him. "Taking it all in for your article?" she asked.

"You did a great job." He acknowledged her with a slight bow.

She swallowed his compliment and asked, "Did you really think I could have done something more creative?"

"Yes," he didn't hesitate to respond. "Now that I've discovered the real Maddie Higgins, your dessert was too simple for someone with your talent."

"What did you expect—a mile-high brownie cake?" she asked, half joking, then added, "Or would you have

...red a new version of my torta di chocolate?" This ...asn't easy for either of them. Being a runner-up might be considered a culinary accomplishment, but winning back Brad's respect was going to take more than a twist of her whisk.

"The mile-high was a clever idea. A real insight to your talent." For a moment a playful sparkle found its way through his tired eyes. "I've heard that your torta is a true dining pleasure." He gave her a sly look. "Without the soap, of course."

"You still can't let that go, can you?" What did she have to do to make him trust her again?

"I'm working on it." He uncrossed his arms and for a moment he looked like he was going to take her hand. "You bringing something to dessert night at Nona's?"

Maddie had been so preoccupied with the show she had almost forgotten about Nona's plan to preview her new line of desserts.

Noticing her surprise he asked, "You're still planning on coming, aren't you?"

"Of course I'll be there. I know how important it is to your grandmother, Lily, and the twins."

"Great, I'll see you then." Brad gave her a friendly peck on the cheek. "Gotta run. My editor is holding the magazine for my article."

She wanted him to believe that she was the same Maddie Higgins he had flirted with in his grandmother's kitchen the day she made the mile-high brownie cake with Lily. It was true things had changed since then. She

"I'm not interested in all that travel. I kinda like what I have here."

"So things are on the mend with you and Brad?" Chloe gave her a quizzical glance. "What did Brad say about all your offers: TV stardom, endorsements, your own baking line?"

"We haven't really had much time to talk." Maddie stared out the window.

"He'll come around. Have you checked out any of the vacant properties Ethan suggested?"

"I don't think I'm financially ready to open a shop." Maddie sighed. "And I'm not TV star material." The possibility of her own show should have made Maddie feel like the cherry on the cake. Instead, she felt like she was in another downward spiral, unsure of her future with Brad.

"There's no shame in doing some endorsements. Even your own baking dishes might be a nice idea. You could promote them from your shop. Talk it over with Brad. He's got lots of experience and connections in the food industry."

Maddie doubted Brad would feel the same way about someone whose face smiled up at him from the bottom of a baking pan.

Maddie didn't think she would like herself very much either. She had come out of her deep hibernation and discovered hidden talents. Doing TV commercials or endorsements was not one of them. She would have to find a better way to raise the money she needed.

She glanced at her watch. "I've got to run. Lily asked

no longer thought he was a horrible monster. Reve[...] no longer occupied her thoughts.

"Hey, Maddie, join us," a crewmember shouted.

"Your public is calling," Brad said. "It's not good to keep them waiting."

Did Brad think that's who she was now, who she had been all along, but just pretending to be someone else? She could think of only one little deviation to who she had been back then. She had been Maddie without her muse and blaming Brad Angelo for its disappearance. Now that she had rediscovered her muse, she had to find a way to prove she was the same Maddie.

Chapter Fifteen

Two days later, Maddie sat next to a hospital bed in the mother/baby unit at County Hospital. She stared with wonder at Chloe and Ethan's perfect baby girl.

"Sounds like you're going to need a publicist." Chloe spoke to Maddie, but her eyes never moved off the delicate face wrapped in a pink cupcake-print blanket.

"Which offer sounds the best to you so far?" she asked.

The minute Maddie had seen the blanket in the gift shop, she knew she had found the perfect present.

"Daytime TV interviews are not my thing. Abe's [...] for a miniseries about chocolate sounds interesting, I'm not TV show material."

"What's the show about?" Chloe asked.

"He wants to spotlight chocolate from the cocoa bea[n] to the finished product. The host would have to travel t[o] several locations just to do one show."

"You sure you'd rather make a go at your own shop instead of riding the wave of your fame?" Chloe cooed at her baby.

---

until she confessed her secret identity. At that point she could have been covered in his favorite chocolate and he wouldn't have cared.

She filled a platter with the best torta di chocolate she had ever made. At the kitchen door Maddie hesitated. Unsure of what awaited her on the other side, she surveyed the guests through the little window. She looked for the twins, Sophia and Emily. They would be easy to spot and Brad wouldn't be far away.

No sign of any of the Angelos in the crowd. The dining room had taken on a new look thanks to a little razzle-dazzle supplied by Tasha. All the desserts were displayed on a round table. Tiered trays filled with nut cakes, mousses, and sponges sat next to trays of Italian cookies.

A tinge of disappointment dampened her high when she didn't see Brad or the twins. She did spot Simon with his camera. Simon and Brad had come to a civilized agreement when Brad's editors suggested he was too close to the event to write about it. It was Brad who suggested a pictorial and recommended the one man who could do the job: Simon. All this was great free publicity for the restaurant.

Maddie entered the dining room. She rearranged some dishes and trays to make room for her dessert. A gentle tap on her shoulder distracted her. Expecting to see Brad, she was disappointed when she discovered Abe standing behind her.

"Are those the infamous tortas di chocolate?" He looked puzzled. "Where's the powdered sugar?"

"Sorry. No powder." Maddie had discussed her anxi with Tasha. She couldn't get herself to bake those choc- olate cakes. Tasha had offered a great alternative for the topping: colorful sugar crystals instead of powdered sugar. Maddie had been so enthused by her vision of the final product, she might have been overzealous in the number of tortas she baked.

The end result was striking. The sugar melted lightly onto the warm cakes, giving the entire tray a magical sparkle. Guests reached around her to add one of the treats to their overfilled plates.

"Your dessert is a success." Abe edged her away from the crowd. "No way I can convince you to accept my offer? Traveling to exotic locations appeals to a lot of people." She thought for a second. Sacrificing a year could give her financial security and recognition. "No, not my thing."

"You got other plans?" Abe asked.

"Something in the works," she lied. Over Abe's shoul- der, Maddie watched Simon, Geraldine, and the twins enjoying her dessert.

Her own shop appeared financially unobtainable at the moment. Without her own TV show there probably wouldn't be any endorsements, but the night was still young.

Abe shrugged. "Sorry to hear that. You would have been an instant TV star." He looked around the crowded room. "Where's that little pastry chef who assisted you?"

Zelda Benjamin

"Lily?" Maddie couldn't believe Abe would be so bold. He couldn't possibly want to offer Lily the TV show and steal her away from Nona right under her nose.

"Yes, that cute little thing with the spiked hair. She's part of a chocolate dynasty. Viewers will love her." Abe turned to leave.

"How fickle is that man?" Maddie said out loud.

"I hope you weren't referring to me." Brad came up behind her.

Maddie felt a lump grow in her throat. She turned to face him.

"No, not you. That Abe, he's a real character," she said.

"One of a kind." One side of his mouth rose in a smile. "I heard he offered you a TV show."

"I turned him down." She took a deep breath and asked, "Did you finish your story?"

"Almost. I need the final who, what, and where about the winner and losers. So far, Sam is staying where he is. Tasha is going to expand her shop." He raised a brow and asked, "You have any special plans?"

"No." At the moment she didn't want to move from this spot. Brad smiled down at her. "Why would I leave?" Her heart beat anxiously in her chest. Did he understand that she wanted to stay because of him? Was he willing to let her into his special group? "I've got everything I need right here."

"That's good." He stepped closer. "Lots of people would be upset if you went tramping around the world."

"Oh, really? Who?" she baited him.

"The twins, Nona . . ." He ran his thumb deliciously up and down her arm. "And me."

He wanted her to stay, but hadn't said so until she told him she had turned Abe down.

Before either of them had a chance to say another word, Nona appeared. Her hands waving in the air, she announced, "Someone just stole my pastry chef."

"Oh, no." Maddie grabbed her chest. He did it. Abe stole Lily from Nona in her own kitchen.

"Who?" Brad resumed his reporter's posture.

"Abe Zukini. What kind of grown man has a name like that?" Nona regained her composure and turned to Maddie.

Maddie saw a strange look in the older woman's eyes and feared the worst. She was about to blame her for the loss of her pastry chef.

But Nona surprised everyone. "Lily's a young girl with lots of talent. It's time for her to move on. I'm sad to see her go, but with her family connections she's perfect for Mr. Zukini's TV show." Her frown turned to a smile. "It will help her when she's ready to take over Peradou Chocolates."

"You're not thinking of going back into the kitchen full time?" Brad asked, obviously concerned for his grandmother. "Are you?"

"No. I'm too old. I can still stuff a few cannolis, but with tonight's success, I couldn't keep up with the dessert orders."

ou're going to need a pastry chef. What will you
do?" Maddie felt responsible.

Nona studied Maddie, then turned to Brad. "What do
you think?"

"She has possibility," Brad responded with a casual
glance at Maddie.

"You want the job?" Nona asked. "That crazy Tony,
he's already talking about expanding. He'd like to start
small. He liked your idea. Maybe a dessert counter and
some tables outside." She winked at Maddie.

"Maddie's idea?" Brad's eyes narrowed suspiciously.
"When did she make that suggestion?"

"The first time you brought her here," Nona said.

Brad threw his hands in the air and said something to
his grandmother in Italian.

Nona smiled and said, "That wasn't the only thing
I knew."

He sighed with exasperation. "You knew back then
Maddie was the soap powder torta chef?"

"Not that day. Lily knew. She told your Uncle Tony, but
swore him to secrecy." Nona looked at Maddie apologetically. "He told me. We're family. We don't keep secrets."

"I'm family too." Brad hesitated before asking, "No
one thought it necessary to share the information with
me?"

Maddie bit her lip. Her thoughts were swimming
through a hazy pool of chocolate sauce. She waited for
him to tell her this was the last straw, but it was Nona
who broke the brief silence.

"A little oversight." Nona shrugged. "It was on a m̶̶
to-know basis." She taped her finger on Brad's ches.
"And you didn't need to know until Maddie was ready
to tell you."

Nona turned toward Maddie. "Want the job?"

Maddie fought to contain her excitement. Her own
dessert counter in a popular restaurant was more than
she'd expected when she'd wondered how the evening
would end. She looked at Brad. If she took the job she
would be a part of his life too. Without his consent she
couldn't accept. He had said he wanted her to stick
around. Did he still mean it?

"You don't need his permission," Nona said.

"But I do." Maddie felt her skin flush. She didn't want
his approval, just a sign that he understood what all this
would mean to them.

Brad placed his hands on her shoulders. "You are full
of surprises, Maddie Higgins." His grip tightened and his
voice became more serious. He pulled her close and whispered, "Do I have to make you family to guarantee there
are no more secrets between us?"

His suggestion sent her heartbeat skyrocketing. "Even-
tually that might be nice," she managed to reply

Nona tapped her on the shoulder. "Is it a deal? You
want to be the pastry chef here?"

Maddie had no desire to back out of Brad's embrace.
She tilted her head and said, "I'll take the job."

"One more thing." Brad released her, took her hand,
and gently pulled her along behind him.